THE ULTIMATE
PHILADELPHIA PHILLIES
TRIVIA BOOK

A Collection of Amazing Trivia Quizzes
and Fun Facts for Die-Hard Phillies Fans!

Ray Walker

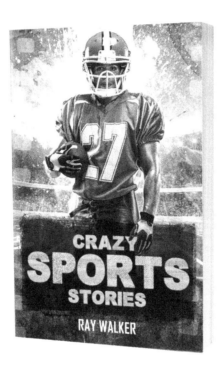

CONTENTS

INTRODUCTION

The Philadelphia Phillies were established in 1883. As one of the oldest teams in Major League Baseball, the Phillies have proven themselves to be a team that fights hard and is a force to be reckoned with in the MLB postseason.

They currently hold two World Series championships, which they won in 1980 and 2008. They have also won the National League Pennant seven times. They are very often a threat in the National League East Division, having won it 11 times total. Oddly enough, they do not yet have a wild card berth to their name.

The Phillies have retired the uniform numbers of Richie Ashburn, Jim Bunning, Mike Schmidt, Steve Carlton, and Robin Roberts. They also have a "Wall of Fame" at Citizens Bank Park to celebrate their past and the players and people who made it all possible.

The thing about baseball is that it is a lot like life. There are good times and bad times, good days and bad days, but you have to do your absolute best to never give up. The Philadelphia Phillies have proven that they refuse to give up and that they will do anything they need to do in order to bring a championship to the City of Brotherly Love.

Winning is more than possible when you have a storied past, as the Phillies do. They have so much captivating history and so many undeniable player legacies to be profoundly proud of.

The Phillies' current home is Citizens Bank Park, which opened in 2004. They play in one of the most difficult divisions in baseball, the National League East, along with the Atlanta Braves, Miami Marlins, New York Mets, and Washington Nationals.

With such a storied team past that goes back generations, you're probably already very knowledgeable as the die-hard Phillies fan that you are. Let's test that knowledge to see if you truly are the World's Biggest Phillies fan.

CHAPTER 1:

ORIGINS AND HISTORY

QUIZ TIME!

1. Which of the following team names did the Phillies franchise once go by?

    a. Quakers
    b. Blue Jays
    c. Eagles
    d. Both A and B

2. In what year was the Philadelphia Phillies franchise established?

    a. 1870
    b. 1883
    c. 1899
    d. 1901

3. The Phillies' current home stadium is Citizens Bank Park.

    a. True
    b. False

4. Which division do the Philadelphia Phillies play in?

    a. American League Central
    b. American League East
    c. National League East
    d. National League Central

5. The Philadelphia Phillies have never won a wild card berth.

    a. True
    b. False

6. How many National League Pennants has the Phillies franchise won (as of the 2020 season)?

    a. 3
    b. 7
    c. 9
    d. 12

7. What is the name of the Phillies' mascot?

    a. Phillie Filly
    b. Phillie Penguin
    c. Phillie Parrot
    d. Phillie Phanatic

8. Who is the longest-tenured manager in Philadelphia Phillies history (as of the 2020 season)?

    a. Larry Bowa
    b. Gene Mauch
    c. Charlie Manuel
    d. Eddie Sawyer

9. What is the name of the Philadelphia Phillies' Triple-A farm team and where is it located?

    a. Lehigh Valley IronPigs
    b. Scranton/Wilkes-Barre RailRiders
    c. Charlotte Knights
    d. Toledo Mud Hens

10. Who was the first manager of the franchise?

    a. Blondie Purcell
    b. Bob Ferguson
    c. Harry Wright
    d. Al Reach

11. The Phillies are the oldest continuous same-name, same-city franchise in American professional sports.

    a. True
    b. False

12. What is the name of the Phillies' current spring training home stadium?

    a. Ed Smith Stadium
    b. First Data Field
    c. Spectrum Field
    d. Hammond Stadium

13. How many appearances has the franchise made in the MLB playoffs (as of the 2020 season)?

    a. 9
    b. 11
    c. 14
    d. 18

14. How many World Series titles have the Phillies won (as of the 2020 season)?

    a. 1
    b. 2
    c. 3
    d. 4

15. The Phillies played in the American League East Division from 1969 through 1975.

    a. True
    b. False

16. What was the first home stadium of the Philadelphia Phillies' franchise?

    a. Connie Mack Stadium
    b. Veterans Stadium
    c. Recreation Park
    d. Baker Bowl

17. As of the 2020 season, how many National League Pennants have the Phillies won?

    a. 3
    b. 5
    c. 7
    d. 9

18. How many National League East Division titles have the Phillies won (as of the 2020 season)?

    a. 6
    b. 11

c. 15

d. 18

19. Which team is NOT currently in the National League East Division with the Phillies?

    a. Miami Marlins

    b. Washington Nationals

    c. New York Mets

    d. Chicago Cubs

20. Of all the teams in the NL East, the Phillies have won their division the most times.

    a. True

    b. False

QUIZ ANSWERS

1. D – Both A and B

2. B – 1883

3. A – True

4. C – National League East

5. A – True

6. B – 7

7. D – Phillie Phanatic

8. B – Gene Mauch

9. A – Lehigh Valley IronPigs

10. B – Bob Ferguson

11. A – True

12. C – Spectrum Field

13. C – 14

14. B – 2

15. B – False (They have always been in the National League East Division.)

16. C – Recreation Park

17. C – 7

18. B – 11

19. D – Chicago Cubs (they were a founding member of the NL East but moved to the NL Central in 1994).

20. B – False (Atlanta Braves)

DID YOU KNOW?

1. The Phillies have had 55 managers: Bob Ferguson, Blondie Purcell, Harry Wright, Jack Clements, Al Reach, Bob Allen, Arthur Irwin, Billy Nash, George Stallings, Bill Shettsline, Chief Zimmer, Hugh Duffy, Billy Murray, Red Dooin, Pat Moran, Jack Coombs, Gavvy Cravath, Bill Donovan, Kaiser Wilhelm, Art Fletcher, Stuffy McInnis, Burt Shotton, Jimmie Wilson, Hans Lobert, Bucky Harris, Freddie Fitzsimmons, Ben Chapman, Dusty Cooke, Eddie Sawyer, Steve O'Neill, Terry Moore, Mayo Smith, Andy Cohen, Gene Mauch, Bob Skinner, George Myatt, Frank Lucchesi, Paul Owens, Danny Ozark, Dallas Green, Pat Corrales, John Felske, Lee Elia, John Vukovich, Nick Leyva, Jim Fregosi, Terry Francona, Larry Bowa, Gary Varsho, Charlie Manuel, Ryne Sandberg, Pete Mackanin, Gabe Kapler, and Joe Girardi.

2. The Phillies' current manager is Joe Girardi. He previously managed the Florida Marlins in 2006 and the New York Yankees from 2008 to 2017. During his playing career as a catcher, he was with the Chicago Cubs, Colorado Rockies, New York Yankees, and the St. Louis Cardinals.

3. Charlie Manuel is the Philadelphia Phillies' all-time winningest manager with a record of 780-636 (.551) W-L%.

4. Robin Roberts was the first Phillie to have his number retired by the team. His number 36 was retired in 1962.

5. The Philadelphia Phillies have hosted three MLB All-Star Games so far. The first one took place in 1952 at Shibe Park, the second in 1976 at Veterans Stadium, and the third in 1996 at Veterans Park. The Phillies are slated to host the 2026 MLB All-Star Game at Citizens Bank Park.

6. Phillies pitchers have thrown 13 no-hitters. The first was thrown by Charles Ferguson in 1885 and the latest was thrown by Cole Hamels in 2015.

7. Two perfect games have been thrown in Phillies franchise history. The first was thrown by Jim Bunning in 1964 and the second was thrown by Roy Halladay in 2010.

8. The Phillies' Double-A farm team is the Reading Fightin' Phils. They have been the Double-A affiliate of the Phillies since 1967. They are currently tied for the longest affiliation in minor-league baseball.

9. The Phillies PA announcer is Dan Baker, who has held the job since the 1972 season.

10. The Phillie Phanatic is a large, furry, green flightless bird. He is originally from the Galápagos Islands and is the Phillies' biggest fan… or "phan."

CHAPTER 2:

JERSEYS AND NUMBERS

QUIZ TIME!

1. The current Phillies logo, team colors, and uniform date back to 1992.

    a. True
    b. False

2. The Phillies and which other team are the only MLB teams to have chain stitching on their chest emblems?

    a. New York Yankees
    b. Los Angeles Dodgers
    c. Toronto Blue Jays
    d. St. Louis Cardinals

3. In 2008, the Phillies introduced an alternate cream-colored uniform for home day games as a tribute to the franchise's 125th anniversary.

    a. True
    b. False

4. Which of the following numbers has NOT been retired by the Philadelphia Phillies (as of the end of the 2020 season)?

    a. 14
    b. 18
    c. 20
    d. 32

5. What uniform number does OF Bryce Harper wear as a member of the Phillies?

    a. 3
    b. 13
    c. 33
    d. 34

6. What uniform number did slugger Mike Schmidt wear during his time with the Phillies?

    a. 20
    b. 22
    c. 27
    d. Both A and B

7. The Phillies are the only team in the MLB who displays the player's number on one sleeve in addition to the usual placement on the back of the jersey.

    a. True
    b. False

8. Who is the only Phillies player to ever wear No. 0?

    a. Al Dark
    b. Rene Gonzales

c. Al Oliver

d. Mitch Williams

9. Which former Phillies legend had his No. 32 retired by the team?

a. Richie Ashburn

b. Jim Bunning

c. Robin Roberts

d. Steve Carlton

10. Throughout the 2009 season, the Phillies wore black circular "HK" patches over the hearts on their uniforms in memory of broadcaster Harry Kalas.

a. True

b. False

11. What are the Philadelphia Phillies' official team colors?

a. Burgundy, white, blue

b. Red, white, blue

c. Red, blue, burgundy

d. Red, white, blue, black

12. Who was the first Phillie to have his uniform number retired by the team?

a. Mike Schmidt

b. Chuck Klein

c. Richie Ashburn

d. Steve Carlton

13. RHP Robin Roberts is the latest to have his number (36) retired by the Phillies, on June 18, 2008.

a. True

b. False

14. What jersey number did Jim Bunning wear as a Phillie?

    a. 14

    b. 17

    c. 38

    d. Both A and C

15. What jersey number did Richie Ashburn wear as a Phillie?

    a. 1

    b. 11

    c. 21

    d. All of the Above

16. What jersey number did Chase Utley wear as a Phillie?

    a. 16

    b. 26

    c. 36

    d. Both A and B

17. What jersey number did Ryan Howard wear as a Phillie?

    a. 6

    b. 12

    c. 24

    d. Both A and B

18. What jersey number did Jimmy Rollins wear as a Phillie?

a. 6

b. 11

c. 29

d. All of the Above

19. What jersey number did Roy Halladay wear as a Phillie?

    a. 32

    b. 34

    c. 52

    d. None of the Above

20. Grover Cleveland Alexander and Chuck Klein are retired by the Phillies, but by letter, not number. The letter "P" represents them and their honor.

    a. True

    b. False

QUIZ ANSWERS

1. A – True

2. D – St. Louis Cardinals

3. A – True

4. B – 18

5. A – 3

6. D – Both A and B. Although No. 20 is retired by the Phillies, Schmidt did wear No. 22 in his rookie season.

7. A – True

8. C – Al Oliver

9. D – Steve Carlton

10. A – True

11. B – Red, white, blue

12. C – Richie Ashburn (Aug. 24, 1979)

13. A – True

14. A – 14

15. A – 1

16. B – 26

17. D – Both A and B

18. D – All of the Above

19. B – 34

20. A – True

DID YOU KNOW?

1. The Phillies are one of only four MLB teams who do not display their city, state, or region on their road jerseys. The other three teams who do not do this are the Los Angeles Angels of Anaheim, St. Louis Cardinals, and the Tampa Bay Rays.

2. In 2017, the Phillies revived their powder blue uniform as an alternate home uniform to be worn on select Thursday games.

3. During spring training, the Phillies wear solid red practice jerseys with red pinstripe pants at home and gray pants on the road. Back in 1977, the Phillies wore maroon V-neck uniforms during spring training.

4. In 1979, the Phillies debuted all-burgundy uniforms with white trimmings called the "Saturday Night Specials." They were only worn once due to outrage from fans. Many described the uniforms as "Pajama-like."

5. In 1994, the Phillies debuted all-blue hats on Opening Day. Players wanted them discontinued because they thought they were bad luck. A compromise was reached and they wore the blue hats for every weekday game and wore their red caps for Sunday games.

6. The Phillies have retired seven players and five numbers. Richie Ashburn's No. 1 was retired on Aug.

24, 1979, Jim Bunning's No. 14 on April 6, 2001, Mike Schmidt's No. 20 on May 26, 1990, Steve Carlton's No. 32 on July 29, 1989, Robin Robert's No. 36 on June 18, 2008. Grover Cleveland Alexander and Chuck Klein both had the letter "P" retired in their honor on April 6, 2001. Of course, Jackie Robinson's No. 42 is retired throughout MLB.

7. The Phillies do plan to retire the late Roy Halladay's No. 34. He will also have a statue in the Third Base Plaza of Citizens Bank Park. Halladay was posthumously named to the National Baseball Hall of Fame in 2019.

8. Three players have worn the No. 99 for the Phillies: Mitch Williams in 1993, Turk Wendell in 2001, and So Taguchi in 2008.

9. Pat Neshek is the only player ever to have worn No. 93 for the Phillies (at least so far). He wore it from 2018 to 2019.

10. Instead of a number on the back of his jersey, the Phillies' mascot, the Phillie Phanatic, has a star where his number would be.

CHAPTER 3:

FAMOUS QUOTES

QUIZ TIME!

1. Which former Phillie once said, "I never want to look in the mirror and say, 'What if? What if I had run harder? What if I had dived for that ground ball'"?

   a. Jimmy Rollins

   b. Mike Schmidt

   c. Steve Carlton

   d. Chase Utley

2. Which current Phillies player once said, "If you don't have dreams, you don't have a life. That's my motto"?

   a. Andrew McCutchen

   b. Bryce Harper

   c. Didi Gregorius

   d. Jake Arrieta

3. Which former Phillie is quoted as saying, "To cure a batting slump, I took my bat to bed with me. I wanted to know my bat a little better"?

a. Jayson Werth
b. Grover Cleveland Alexander
c. Richie Ashburn
d. Matt Stairs

4. Which former Phillie once said, "Underdog. That's something we've become accustomed to, playing in Philadelphia. We're always the underdog"?

a. Pete Rose
b. Jimmy Rollins
c. Tug McGraw
d. Shane Victorino

5. Which former Phillies pitcher is quoted as saying, "I've always tried to work hard. I'm not trying to show anybody up or do something spectacular for attention"?

a. Curt Schilling
b. Randy Wolf
c. Roy Halladay
d. Ryan Madson

6. Which former Phillie is quoted as saying, "I don't think I can get into my deep inner thoughts about hitting. It's like talking about religion"?

a. Mike Schmidt
b. Hunter Pence
c. Jim Thome
d. Pete Rose

7. Which former Phillies pitcher is Randy Johnson referring to?

8. "I had a long conversation with _____. He told me that on the days he pitched, he felt it was his responsibility to make everyone around him better, to lift his teammates. That's what I try to do." – Randy Johnson

   a. Jim Bunning
   b. Tug McGraw
   c. Jim Kaat
   d. Steve Carlton

9. Former Phillies OF Chuck Klein once said, "A life is not important except in the impact it has on other lives."

   a. True
   b. False

10. Which former Phillies manager is quoted as saying, "There's no pressure in baseball. Pressure is when the doctor is getting ready to cut you, take your heart out, and put it on a table"?

    a. Mayo Smith
    b. Charlie Manuel
    c. Dallas Green
    d. Jim Fregosi

11. Which former Phillies manager is quoted as saying, "You can't lead anyone else further than you have gone yourself"?

a. Gene Mauch

b. Terry Francona

c. Danny Ozark

d. Eddie Sawyer

12. Which Phillie is quoted as saying, "I'd walk through hell in a gasoline suit to play baseball"?

a. Mike Schmidt

b. Bryce Harper

c. Pete Rose

d. Joe Blanton

13. Which current MLB star is quoted as saying, "I grew up a Phillies fan. Me and my buddies tailgated a couple of times when they won the World Series. I like just being in that atmosphere"?

a. Aaron Judge

b. Anthony Rizzo

c. Nolan Arenado

d. Mike Trout

14. Which former Phillies player is quoted as saying, "I've talked to guys who have played for the Phillies and gone on to other organizations and the grass isn't always greener on the other side"?

a. John Kruk

b. Ryne Sandberg

c. Chase Utley

d. Ryan Howard

15. Which former Phillie is quoted as saying, "Rooting is following and I don't do that, but I'd like to see the Phillies win because I love Philadelphia"?

    a. Steve Carlton
    b. Lenny Dykstra
    c. Mike Schmidt
    d. Cole Hamels

16. Which former Phillies player is quoted as saying, "If I had to give advice about parents, it would be this: Value your relationships with them. Those relationships are what you stand for. Not only are we blessed to wear a uniform that says PHILLIES on the front, but we have our names on the back. That name means you're playing for your family"?

    a. Jamie Moyer
    b. Jim Thome
    c. Terry Mulholland
    d. Mitch Williams

17. Phillies pitcher Grover Alexander Cleveland once said, "Never allow the fear of striking out keep you from playing the game."

    a. True
    b. False

18. Which former Phillie is quoted as saying, "My father left me with a saying that I've carried my entire life and tried to pass on to our kids, 'Tough times don't last, tough people do'"?

a. John Kruk

b. Jim Bunning

c. Curt Schilling

d. Richie Ashburn

19. Which former Phillies player once said, "I can't stand satisfaction. To me, greatness comes from that quest for perfection"?

    a. Mike Schmidt

    b. Steve Carlton

    c. John Kruk

    d. Pete Rose

20. Which former Phillie once said, "You'd be surprised how many shortcomings can be overcome by hustle"?

    a. Mike Schmidt

    b. Pete Rose

    c. Steve Carlton

    d. Chase Utley

21. Former Phillie Scott Rolen once said, "I enjoy coming to the ballpark every day. I don't go to work. I come here to play."

    a. True

    b. False

QUIZ ANSWERS

1. D – Chase Utley
2. B – Bryce Harper
3. C – Richie Ashburn
4. B – Jimmy Rollins
5. C – Roy Halladay
6. A – Mike Schmidt
7. D – Steve Carson
8. B – False, Jackie Robinson
9. B – Charlie Manuel
10. A – Gene Mauch
11. C – Pete Rose
12. D – Mike Trout
13. C – Chase Utley
14. A – Steve Carlton
15. B – Jim Thome
16. B – False, Babe Ruth
17. C – Curt Schilling
18. A – Mike Schmidt
19. B – Pete Rose
20. A – True

DID YOU KNOW?

1. "Pete Rose is the most likable arrogant person I've ever met." – Mike Schmidt

2. "You feel like a rock star in some ways." – Cole Hamels on starting on Opening Day

3. "On some nights, you could totally predict that he was going to do something special." – A.J. Burnett on Roy Halladay

4. "I remember Reggie Jackson said: 'They don't boo nobodies.' I took that into consideration when I was 15, 16 years old." – Bryce Harper

5. "When Steve Carlton and I die, we're gonna be buried 60'6" apart." – Tim McCarver

6. "It's about focusing on the fight and not the fright." – Robin Roberts

7. "I avoided as much work as possible in the classroom but did all the work possible on the ballfield." – Chuck Klein

8. "I wish I'd known early what I had to learn late." – Richie Ashburn

9. "That's a clown question, bro." – Bryce Harper

10. "To both of the teams that we were blessed to be a part of — the Blue Jays and the Phillies. Thank you for

allowing us to grow up, to fail over and over, and finally learn how to succeed within your organizations. There were some really amazing years but there were some really tough ones, too, and you never gave up on him.

11. "More than anything, he would want both organizations to know that they hold a huge place in our heart and always will. Evidence of their love for us and our love for them, as well, was shown all week as they came together as one to celebrate Roy — and that means the world to me. To both organizations, I can't thank you enough.

12. "I think that Roy would want everyone to know that people are not perfect. We are all imperfect and flawed in one way or another. We all struggle, but with hard work, humility, and dedication, imperfect people can still have perfect moments. Roy was blessed in his life and in his career to have some perfect moments, but I believe that they were only possible because of the man he strived to be, the teammate that he was, and the people that he was so blessed to be on the field with." – Brandy Halladay's speech at the late Roy Halladay's National Baseball Hall of Fame Induction Ceremony

CHAPTER 4:

CATCHY NICKNAMES

QUIZ TIME!

1. Which nickname did P Steve Carlton go by?

   a. Stevey

   b. Carl

   c. Lefty

   d. Righty

2. Carlos Ruiz's nickname is "Chooch."

   a. True

   b. False

3. What was Roy Halladay's real first name?

   a. John

   b. Ryan

   c. Michael

   d. Harry

4. What was Roy Halladay's famous nickname?

   a. Hally

   b. Doc

c. Roy-Hall

d. Uncle

5. Which is NOT a nickname that has been applied to the Phillies as a team?

   a. The Phils

   b. The Fightin' Phils

   c. The Red Pinstripes

   d. The Lilies

6. Which nickname did Lenny Dykstra NOT go by?

   a. The Dude

   b. The Len Man

   c. Nails

   d. Dr. Dirt

7. Jimmy Rollins' nickname was "J-Roll."

   a. True

   b. False

8. Which nickname did Shane Victorino go by?

   a. Vic

   b. The Flyin' Hawaiian

   c. Super Shane

   d. Aloha

9. What nickname did former Phillie Richie Ashburn go by?

   a. Whitey

   b. Put-Put

c. Ashy

d. Both A and B

10. What is Mitch Williams' nickname?

   a. Willie

   b. Mitchie

   c. Wild Thing

   d. Crazy Mitch

11. What was Pete Rose's nickname?

   a. Rosie

   b. Prose

   c. Pete Hustle

   d. Charlie Hustle

12. Roy Halladay got the nickname "Doc" because he was a pediatrician during the baseball offseason.

   a. True

   b. False

13. What is Gary Matthew's nickname?

   a. Big G

   b. Sir

   c. Sarge

   d. Matty

14. What is Greg Luzinski's nickname?

   a. The Bull

   b. The Scorpion

   c. The Bulldog

   d. The Lion

15. Garry Maddox went by the nickname "The Secretary of Defense."

    a. True
    b. False

16. Which nickname was given to former Phillies closer Tug McGraw?

    a. TMG
    b. The Graw Man
    c. T-Graw
    d. Tugger

17. Former Phillies third baseman Willie Jones went by the nickname "Puddin' Head."

    a. True
    b. False

18. What nickname did former Phillies first baseman Dick Stuart go by?

    a. D-Stew
    b. Dr. Stewart
    c. Dr. Strangeglove
    d. Dr. Goldfinger

19. What was the nickname of former Phillies OF Bake McBride?

    a. The Baker Man
    b. Shake n Bake
    c. Bride n Groom
    d. Baker's Dozen

20. Chase Utley's nickname is "The Man."

    a. True

    b. False

QUIZ ANSWERS

1. C – Lefty
2. A – True
3. D – Harry
4. B – Doc
5. D – The Lilies
6. B – The Len Man
7. A – True
8. B – The Flyin' Hawaiian
9. D – Both A and B
10. C – Wild Thing
11. D – Charlie Hustle
12. B – False
13. C – Sarge
14. A – The Bull
15. A – True
16. D – Tugger
17. A – True
18. C – Dr. Strangeglove
19. B – Shake n Bake
20. A – True

DID YOU KNOW?

1. Former Phillie Pat Burrell was known as "Pat the Bat."

2. Former Phillie Mickey Morandini had the interesting nickname, "Dandy Little Glove Man."

3. Brad Lidge's nickname is "Lights Out."

4. Former Phillie Kevin Saucier was given the nickname "Hot Sauce" by fans.

5. Ryan Howard's nickname is "The Big Piece."

6. Former Phillie John Kruk goes by the nickname "Krukker."

7. Cole Hamels' nickname is "Hollywood."

8. Former Phillie Larry Bowa's nickname is "Gnat."

9. Mike Schmidt's nickname is simply "Schmitty."

10. Former Phillies catcher Darren Daulton's nickname is "Dutch."

CHAPTER 5:

SCHMITTY

QUIZ TIME!

1. What is Mike Schmidt's full name?

    a. Michael Gary Schmidt
    b. Michael James Schmidt
    c. Michael Edward Schmidt
    d. Michael Jack Schmidt

2. Mike Schmidt played his entire 18-season MLB career with the Philadelphia Phillies.

    a. True
    b. False

3. Where was Mike Schmidt born?

    a. Philadelphia, Pennsylvania
    b. San Diego, California
    c. Dayton, Ohio
    d. Portland, Oregon

4. When is Mike Schmidt's birthday?

   a. September 27, 1946

   b. September 27, 1949

   c. November 27, 1946

   d. November 27, 1949

5. Mike Schmidt was elected to the National Baseball Hall of Fame in 1995 with 96.5% of the vote.

   a. True

   b. False

6. On April 17, 1976, how many home runs did Mike Schmidt hit in one game?

   a. 3

   b. 4

   c. 5

   d. 6

7. How many MLB All-Star Games was Mike Schmidt named to during his career?

   a. 6

   b. 8

   c. 12

   d. 14

8. Mike Schmidt was a 3x National League MVP (1980, 1981, 1986).

   a. True

   b. False

9. Mike Schmidt was drafted by the Phillies in what round of the 1971 MLB draft?

    a. 1st
    b. 2nd
    c. 10th
    d. 15th

10. How many times did Mike Schmidt lead the National League in home runs?

    a. 5 times
    b. 8 times
    c. 10 times
    d. 12 times

11. How many times did Mike Schmidt lead the National League in RBI?

    a. 2 times
    b. 3 times
    c. 4 times
    d. 5 times

12. Mike Schmidt was named the 1980 World Series MVP.

    a. True
    b. False

13. How many Gold Glove Awards did Mike Schmidt win?

    a. 6
    b. 7
    c. 8
    d. 10

14. How many Silver Slugger Awards did Mike Schmidt win?

    a. 3
    b. 5
    c. 6
    d. 9

15. How many home runs did Mike Schmidt hit?

    a. 521
    b. 548
    c. 601
    d. 648

16. What is Mike Schmidt's career batting average?

    a. .250
    b. .259
    c. .267
    d. .299

17. Mike Schmidt stole 174 bases.

    a. True
    b. False

18. What year was Mike Schmidt's uniform number retired by the Phillies?

    a. 1990
    b. 1991
    c. 1992
    d. 1993

19. Where did Mike Schmidt attend college?

    a. University of Cincinnati
    b. Bowling Green State University
    c. Ohio State University
    d. Ohio University

20. Mike Schmidt made his MLB debut against the New York Mets and played his final MLB game against the Mets.

    a. True
    b. False

QUIZ ANSWERS

1. D – Michael Jack Schmidt

2. A – True

3. C – Dayton, Ohio

4. B – September 27, 1949

5. A – True

6. B – 4

7. C – 12

8. A – True

9. B – 2nd

10. B – 8 times (1974, 1975, 1976, 1980, 1981, 1983, 1984, 1986)

11. C – 4 times (1980, 1981, 1984, 1986)

12. A – True

13. D – 10

14. C – 6

15. B – 548

16. C – .267

17. A – True

18. A – 1990 (the year after he retired!)

19. D – Ohio University

20. B – False (he debuted against the Mets but his final game was against the San Francisco Giants.)

DID YOU KNOW?

1. In 2006, Mike Schmidt wrote a book called, Clearing the Bases: Juiced Players, Monster Salaries, Sham Records, and a Hall of Famer's Search for the Soul of Baseball.

2. Since 2002, Mike Schmidt has worked as a hitting coach with the Phillies during spring training.

3. In 2001, Mike Schmidt debuted a fishing tournament called, "Mike Schmidt Winner's Circle Invitational." The tournament helps raise money for cystic fibrosis.

4. In 2008, Mike Schmidt introduced a wine named Mike Schmidt 548 Zinfandel. The 548 is a reference to his career home runs stat. All proceeds went to cystic fibrosis.

5. Mike Schmidt battled Stage 3 melanoma but is now cancer-free. Wear sunscreen every day, people!

6. The most home runs Mike Schmidt hit in one season was in 1980 when he hit a whopping 48 home runs in 150 games played and 548 at-bats. He also had his highest RBI total for a season that year with 121. The Phils just so happened to win the World Series in 1980.

7. Mike Schmidt's batting average was an impressive .316 in 1981.

8. "Philadelphia is the only city where you can experience the thrill of victory and the agony of reading about it the next day." – Mike Schmidt

9. "There are things as a coach you can teach, but natural ability like the raw power [Schmidt] had is a rare gift you see maybe once in a lifetime." – Bob Wren, Mike Schmidt's coach at Ohio University

10. "If I had to do it all over again, I'd do it in Philadelphia. The only thing I'd change would be me. I would be less sensitive, more outgoing, and appreciative of what you expected from me." – Mike Schmidt in his National Baseball Hall of Fame induction speech

CHAPTER 6:

STATISTICALLY SPEAKING

QUIZ TIME!

1. Mike Schmidt holds the Philadelphia Phillies franchise record for the most home runs. How many did he hit?

    a. 382

    b. 450

    c. 548

    d. 568

2. Pitcher Steve Carlton has the most wins in Philadelphia Phillies franchise history with 241.

    a. True

    b. False

3. How many times have the Philadelphia Phillies appeared in the playoffs?

    a. 10

    b. 12

    c. 14

    d. 17

4. Which former Phillies batter holds the top FOUR single-season records for strikeouts with 199 in 2007 and 2008, 190 in 2014, and 186 in 2009?

   a. Mike Schmidt
   b. Jim Thome
   c. Marlon Byrd
   d. Ryan Howard

5. Which pitcher has the most strikeouts in Phillies franchise history with a whopping 3,031?

   a. Cole Hamels
   b. Steve Carlton
   c. Robin Roberts
   d. Curt Schilling

6. Who has the most stolen bases in Phillies franchise history with 510?

   a. Billy Hamilton
   b. Jimmy Rollins
   c. Ed Delahanty
   d. Sherry Magee

7. José Mesa holds the record for most saves in Phillies history with 123.

   a. True
   b. False

8. Who is the Phillies' all-time winningest manager?

   a. Kaiser Wilhelm
   b. Eddie Sawyer

c. Charlie Manuel

d. Danny Ozark

9. Which player holds the Phillies franchise record for home runs in a single season with 58?

    a. Ryan Howard

    b. Mike Schmidt

    c. Jim Thome

    d. Cy Williams

10. Who holds the single-season Phillies record with 254 hits?

    a. Richie Ashburn

    b. Sam Thompson

    c. Chuck Klein

    d. Lefty O'Doul

11. Which two players are tied for the single-season Phillies record for double plays grounded into with 25 each?

    a. Del Ennis and David Bell

    b. Del Ennis and Ted Sizemore

    c. Glenn Wilson and Ted Sizemore

    d. David Bell and Ted Sizemore

12. Chase Utley holds the record for the most sacrifice flies in Phillies history with 108.

    a. True

    b. False

13. Steve Carlton threw how many of the wildest pitches in Phillies franchise history?

a. 64

b. 71

c. 120

d. 145

14. Sam Thompson holds the Phillies single-season record for most triples. How many did he hit in his record 1894 season?

    a. 28

    b. 23

    c. 21

    d. 20

15. Which hitter has the most walks in Phillies franchise history with 1,507?

    a. Bobby Abreu

    b. Jimmy Rollins

    c. Chase Utley

    d. Mike Schmidt

16. Which Phillies hitter holds the all-time franchise record for best overall batting average at .360?

    a. Nap Lajoie

    b. Billy Hamilton

    c. Elmer Flick

    d. Spud Davis

17. Mike Schmidt has the most games played as a Phillie and holds the Phillies record for WAR, plate appearances, runs scored, total bases, home runs, RBI, walks, extra-

base hits, sacrifice flies, intentional walks, and times on base.

   a. True

   b. False

18. Mike Schmidt has the most plate appearances of all time in Phillies franchise history. How many did he have?

   a. 9,511

   b. 9,876

   c. 10,062

   d. 10,099

19. Which pitcher holds the Phillies franchise record for most saves in a single season with 45?

   a. Mitch Williams

   b. Jonathan Papelbon

   c. Brad Lidge

   d. José Mesa

20. Robin Roberts holds the Phillies franchise record for most losses with 199.

   a. True

   b. False

QUIZ ANSWERS

1. C – 548
2. A – True
3. C – 14
4. D – Ryan Howard
5. B – Steve Carlton
6. A – Billy Hamilton
7. B – False, Jonathan Papelbon
8. C – Charlie Manuel (780-636, .551 W-L%)
9. A – Ryan Howard (2006)
10. D – Lefty O'Doul (1929)
11. B – Del Ennis (1950) and Ted Sizemore (1977)
12. B – False, Mike Schmidt
13. C – 120
14. A – 28
15. D – Mike Schmidt
16. B – Billy Hamilton
17. A – True
18. C – 10, 062
19. D – José Mesa (2002)
20. A – True

DID YOU KNOW?

1. Robin Roberts threw the most innings in Phillies franchise history with 3,739.1. Coming in second is Steve Carlton with 3,697.1 innings.

2. Tuck Turner had the best single-season batting average in Phillies franchise history at .418 in 1894. Sam Thompson comes in the second spot with a batting average of .415 the same season.

3. Chase Utley holds the Phillies franchise record for stolen base percentage with 88.57% success. Billy Hamilton holds the Phillies franchise record for stolen bases with 510. Richie Ashburn holds the Phillies franchise record for the most times caught stealing with 100.

4. Mike Schmidt has the most extra-base hits in Phillies franchise history with 1,015. Second on the list is Jimmy Rollins with 806.

5. Jim Thome holds the Phillies franchise record for at-bats per home run with 13.3. This means that during his time with Philadelphia, Thome hit a home run about every 13-14 at-bats.

6. Aaron Nola holds the Phillies franchise record for strikeouts per 9 innings pitched with 9.743, meaning that he recorded about 9-10 strikeouts in every 9 innings that he pitched for the team.

7. Pitcher Tom Vickery holds the single-season Phillies record for the most hit by pitches with 29 in 1890.

8. Del Ennis and Granny Hamner are tied for the Phillies franchise record for double plays grounded into with 171 each.

9. Kid Gleason holds the Phillies single-season record for wins with 38 in 1890. Second on the list is Pete Alexander with 33 in 1916.

10. John Coleman holds the Phillies record for the most losses pitched in a single season with 48 in 1883. Charlie Ferguson is second on the list with 25 in 1884.

CHAPTER 7:

THE TRADE MARKET

QUIZ TIME!

1. On February 25, 1972, the Philadelphia Phillies traded RHP Rick Wise to the St. Louis Cardinals for which player?

   a. Woodie Fryman
   b. Ken Reynolds
   c. Steve Carlton
   d. Jim Nash

2. On December 16, 2009, the Phillies traded C Travis d'Arnaud, RHP Kyle Drabek, and OF Michael Taylor to the St. Louis Cardinals in exchange for cash and which player?

   a. Jamie Moyer
   b. Roy Halladay
   c. J.A. Happ
   d. Roy Oswalt

3. The Philadelphia Phillies have NEVER made a trade with the Colorado Rockies.

    a. True
    b. False

4. On April 2, 1992, the Philadelphia Phillies traded RHP Jason Grimsley to the Houston Astros in exchange for which player?

    a. Curt Schilling
    b. Terry Mulholland
    c. Greg Mathews
    d. Mitch Williams

5. The Philadelphia Phillies have made only six trades with the Arizona Diamondbacks all time (as of the end of the 2019 season).

    a. True
    b. False

6. In what year did the Philadelphia Phillies acquire RHP Jim Bunning and C Gus Triandos from the Detroit Tigers?

    a. 1960
    b. 1961
    c. 1963
    d. 1965

7. On November 18, 1997, the Philadelphia Phillies traded SS Kevin Stocker to the Tampa Bay Devil Rays in exchange for which player?

a. Mark Lewis

b. Doug Glanville

c. Scott Rolen

d. Bobby Abreu

8. Which team traded LHP Cliff Lee to the Philadelphia Phillies on July 29, 2009?

a. Cleveland Indians

b. Texas Rangers

c. New York Mets

d. Seattle Mariners

9. On July 17, 2008, the Philadelphia Phillies traded Josh Outman, Adrian Cardenas, and Matthew Spencer to the Oakland A's in exchange for which player?

a. Adam Eaton

b. Jimmy Rollins

c. Matt Stairs

d. Joe Blanton

10. The Philadelphia Phillies have only made six trades with the Miami Marlins (as of the end of the 2019 season).

a. True

b. False

11. On July 29, 2010, the Philadelphia Phillies traded Anthony Gose, J.A. Happ, and Jonathan Villar to the Houston Astros in exchange for _____.

a. J.C. Romero

b. Raul Ibañez

    c. Roy Oswalt

    d. Placido Polanco

12. The Philadelphia Phillies have made only six trades with the Kansas City Royals (as of the end of the 2019 season).

    a. True

    b. False

13. How many trades have the Philadelphia Phillies made with the San Diego Padres all time (as of the 2019 season)?

    a. 5

    b. 10

    c. 15

    d. 20

14. The Philadelphia Phillies NEVER traded Ryan Howard.

    a. True

    b. False

15. At the trade deadline in 2015, the Philadelphia Phillies traded Cole Hamels and Jake Diekman, along with cash, to which team in exchange for Jorge Alfaro, Alec Asher, Jerad Eickhoff, Matt Harrison, Jake Thompson, and Nick Williams?

    a. Chicago Cubs

    b. Toronto Blue Jays

    c. Los Angeles Dodgers

    d. Texas Rangers

16. On July 29, 2002, the Philadelphia Phillies traded Doug Nickle, this player, and cash to the St. Louis Cardinals in exchange for Mike Timlin, Bud Smith, and which player?

    a. Scott Rolen, J.D. Drew
    b. Doug Glanville, J.D. Drew
    c. Scott Rolen, Placido Polanco
    d. Doug Glanville, Placido Polanco

17. How many trades have the Philadelphia Phillies made with the Los Angeles Dodgers (as of the 2019 season)?

    a. 5
    b. 10
    c. 15
    d. 20

18. On July 26, 2000, the Philadelphia Phillies traded Curt Schilling to which team in exchange for Omar Daal, Nelson Figueroa, Travis Lee, and Vicente Padilla?

    a. Arizona Diamondbacks
    b. Boston Red Sox
    c. Baltimore Orioles
    d. Houston Astros

19. On December 6, 2006, the Philadelphia Phillies traded Gio Gonzalez and Gavin Floyd to which team in exchange for Freddy Garcia?

    a. Oakland Athletics
    b. Washington Nationals

c. Chicago White Sox

d. Milwaukee Brewers

20. In 1966, the Phillies traded Fergie Jenkins to the Chicago Cubs.

a. True

b. False

QUIZ ANSWERS

1. C – Steve Carlton

2. B – Roy Halladay

3. B – False (four trades as of the end of the 2019 season)

4. A – Curt Schilling

5. A – True

6. C – 1963

7. D – Bobby Abreu

8. A – Cleveland Indians

9. D – Joe Blanton

10. A – True

11. C – Roy Oswalt

12. A – True

13. C – 15

14. A – True

15. D – Texas Rangers

16. C – Scott Rolen, Placido Polanco

17. D – 20

18. A – Arizona Diamondbacks

19. C – Chicago White Sox

20. A – True

DID YOU KNOW?

1. On November 7, 2007, the Philadelphia Phillies traded OF Michael Bourn, RHP Geoff Geary, and INF Mike Costanzo to the Houston Astros in exchange for RHP Brad Lidge and INF Eric Bruntlett.

2. On June 18, 1989, the Philadelphia Phillies traded INF/OF Juan Samuel to the New York Mets in exchange for OF Lenny Dykstra, RHP Roger McDowell, and Tom Edens.

3. On February 23, 1979, the Philadelphia Phillies traded INF Ted Sizemore, OF Jerry Martin, C Barry Foote, RHP Derek Botelho, and RHP Henry Mack to the Chicago Cubs in exchange for 2B Manny Trillo, OF Greg Gross, and C Dave Rader.

4. On December 26, 1917, the Philadelphia Phillies traded OF Dode Paskert to the Chicago Cubs in exchange for OF Cy Williams. Cy Williams supposedly did not get along with the Cubs manager, Fred Mitchell.

5. Curt Flood viewed Philadelphia as a racist city and refused to accept a trade to the Phillies from the St. Louis Cardinals in 1969.

6. In 1958, the Philadelphia Phillies traded P Jack Sanford to the San Francisco Giants in exchange for C Valmy Thomas and P Ruben Gomez.

7. In 1983, the Philadelphia Phillies traded P Willie Hernandez and 1B Dave Bergman to the Detroit Tigers in exchange for C John Wockenfuss and OF Glenn Wilson.

8. In 1917, the Philadelphia Phillies traded P Grover Cleveland Alexander and C Bill Kiefer to the Chicago Cubs in exchange for P Mike Prendergast, C Pickles Dillhoefer, and $60,000. Owner William Baker needed money and feared he would lose Alexander to the WWI draft anyway.

9. In 1982, the Philadelphia Phillies traded 2B Ryne Sandberg and SS Larry Bowa to the Chicago Cubs in exchange for SS Ivan DeJesus.

10. In February of 2019, the Philadelphia Phillies signed free agent OF Bryce Harper to a 13-year, $330 million contract. He is among the highest-paid baseball players of all time.

CHAPTER 8:

DRAFT DAY

QUIZ TIME!

1. Which MLB team drafted former Phillie Jim Thome in the 13th round of the 1989 MLB draft?

    a. Baltimore Orioles

    b. Chicago White Sox

    c. Minnesota Twins

    d. Cleveland Indians

2. With the 17th overall pick in the first round of the 2002 MLB draft, the Philadelphia Phillies selected which player?

    a. Cory Lidle

    b. Cole Hamels

    c. Ryan Madson

    d. Kyle Lohse

3. The Philadelphia Phillies selected 1B Ryan Howard in the 5th round of the 2001 MLB draft from which college?

    a. San Diego State University

    b. University of Missouri

c. Missouri State University

d. Sacramento State University

4. With which overall pick in the first round of the 1995 MLB draft did the Toronto Blue Jays select RHP Roy Halladay?

    a. 1st

    b. 7th

    c. 10th

    d. 17th

5. With the 2nd overall pick in the first round of the 1997 MLB draft, the Philadelphia Phillies selected OF J.D. Drew from which school?

    a. Florida State University

    b. University of Florida

    c. Oregon State University

    d. University of Oregon

6. With the 15th overall pick in the first round of the 2000 MLB draft, the Philadelphia Phillies selected which player out of UCLA?

    a. Chase Utley

    b. Ryan Howard

    c. Bobby Abreu

    d. Doug Glanville

7. The Philadelphia Phillies drafted Bryce Harper with the first overall pick in the 2010 MLB draft.

    a. True

    b. False

8. LHP Jamie Moyer was drafted in the 6th round of the 1984 MLB draft by which team?

    a. Baltimore Orioles

    b. Seattle Mariners

    c. Texas Rangers

    d. Chicago Cubs

9. Mike Schmidt was drafted by the Philadelphia Phillies in what round of the 1971 MLB draft?

    a. 1st

    b. 2nd

    c. 5th

    d. 8th

10. Marlon Byrd was drafted by the Philadelphia Phillies in the 10th round of the 1999 MLB draft.

    a. True

    b. False

11. In the first round of the 2005 MLB draft, the Pittsburgh Pirates selected current Phillies outfielder Andrew McCutchen at which place overall?

    a. 1st

    b. 4th

    c. 7th

    d. 11th

12. John Mabry was drafted by the Philadelphia Phillies in the 6th round of the 1991 MLB draft.

    a. True

    b. False

13. With the first overall pick in the first round of the 1998 MLB draft, the Philadelphia Phillies chose which player out of the University of Miami?

    a. Travis Lee
    b. Doug Glanville
    c. Pat Burrell
    d. Scott Rolen

14. The Philadelphia Phillies selected SS Jimmy Rollins in the 2nd round of the MLB draft in which year?

    a. 1994
    b. 1995
    c. 1996
    d. 1998

15. RHP A.J. Burnett was drafted by which team in the 8th round of the 1995 MLB draft?

    a. Florida Marlins
    b. New York Yankees
    c. Pittsburgh Pirates
    d. New York Mets

16. Third baseman Scott Rolen was drafted in the 2nd round of the 1993 MLB draft by which team?

    a. Philadelphia Phillies
    b. St. Louis Cardinals
    c. Cincinnati Reds
    d. Toronto Blue Jays

17. With the 37th overall pick in the first round of the 2007 MLB draft, the Philadelphia Phillies selected which player?

   a. Carlos Ruiz
   b. Travis d'Arnaud
   c. John Mayberry
   d. Placido Polanco

18. RHP Ryan Madson was drafted by the Philadelphia Phillies in which round of the 1998 MLB draft?

   a. 3rd
   b. 7th
   c. 9th
   d. 12th

19. RHP Joe Blanton was drafted in the first round, 24th overall in the 2002 MLB draft by which team?

   a. Los Angeles Dodgers
   b. Kansas City Royals
   c. Pittsburgh Pirates
   d. Oakland A's

20. With the 3rd overall pick in the 1974 MLB draft, the Philadelphia Phillies chose OF Lonnie Smith.

   a. True
   b. False

QUIZ ANSWERS

1. D – Cleveland Indians

2. B – Cole Hamels

3. C – Missouri State University

4. D – 17th

5. A – Florida State University

6. A – Chase Utley

7. B – False, Washington Nationals

8. D – Chicago Cubs

9. B – 2nd

10. A – True

11. D – 11th

12. B – False, St. Louis Cardinals

13. C – Pat Burrell

14. C – 1996

15. D – New York Mets

16. A – Philadelphia Phillies

17. B – Travis d' Arnaud

18. C – 9th

19. D – Oakland A's

20. A – True

DID YOU KNOW?

1. The New York Mets selected former Phillies CF Lenny Dykstra in the 13th round of the 1981 MLB draft.

2. The Chicago Cubs drafted former Phillies CF Doug Glanville in the 1st round, 12th overall, in the 1991 MLB draft.

3. The Boston Red Sox drafted former Phillies RHP Curt Schilling in the 2nd round of the 1986 MLB draft.

4. The St. Louis Cardinals drafted former Phillies INF Placido Polanco in the 19th round of the 1994 MLB draft.

5. The Los Angeles Dodgers drafted former Phillies OF Shane Victorino in the 6th round of the 1999 MLB draft.

6. The Baltimore Orioles drafted former Phillies OF Jayson Werth in the first round, 22nd overall in the 1997 MLB draft.

7. The Minnesota Twins drafted former Phillies LHP J.C. Romero in the 21st round of the 1997 MLB draft.

8. The Philadelphia Phillies drafted LHP J.A. Happ in the 3rd round of the 2004 MLB draft out of Northwestern University.

9. The Montreal Expos drafted former Phillies LHP Cliff Lee in the 4th round of the 2000 MLB draft.

10. The Baltimore Orioles drafted current Phillies RHP Jake Arrieta in the 5th round of the 2007 MLB draft.

CHAPTER 9:

ODDS AND ENDS

QUIZ TIME!

1. Ryan Howard appeared on which TV sitcom that featured a character with the same name?

    a. Parks and Recreation
    b. The Office
    c. Brooklyn Nine Nine
    d. New Girl

2. Ryan Howard also appeared in an episode of *Entourage* in which he played himself.

    a. True
    b. False

3. Bryce Harper is a fan of which NHL team?

    a. San Jose Sharks
    b. Philadelphia Flyers
    c. Washington Capitals
    d. Vegas Golden Knights

4. Cole Hamels' wife Heidi was a contestant on which TV reality show?

    a. Big Brother
    b. American Ninja Warrior
    c. Survivor
    d. The Amazing Race

5. Shane Victorino was on an episode of which TV show, playing a character named Shaun?

    a. Hawaii Five-0
    b. CSI
    c. Law and Order SVU
    d. NCIS

6. Andrew McCutchen proposed to his longtime girlfriend, Maria on which talk show?

    a. The Tonight Show with Jimmy Fallon
    b. The Late Late Show with James Corden
    c. The View
    d. The Ellen DeGeneres Show

7. Chase Utley and Ryan Howard appeared on an episode of *It's Always Sunny in Philadelphia*, playing themselves in 2010.

    a. True
    b. False

8. Jamie Moyer and his ex-wife, Karen were introduced by which famous baseball broadcaster?

    a. Vin Scully
    b. Bob Uecker

c. Harry Caray

d. Tim McCarver

9. Hunter Pence proposed to his girlfriend Alexis at which famous theme park?

a. Disneyland

b. Walt Disney World

c. Universal Studios Hollywood

d. Knott's Berry Farm

10. Pat Burrell had an English bulldog who was featured in the Phillies' 2008 World Series parade and was named what?

a. Prince

b. Sinatra

c. Elvis

d. Bowie

11. Which famous MLB player is the godfather of Placido Polanco's son Ishmael?

a. Albert Pujols

b. Robinson Cano

c. José Altuve

d. Manny Machado

12. Country singer Tim McGraw is the son of former Phillies pitcher Tug McGraw.

a. True

b. False

13. Lenny Dykstra's son, Cutter is in a relationship with which actress?

    a. Dakota Johnson
    b. Lea Michele
    c. Anna Kendrick
    d. Jamie Lynn Sigler

14. Which former Phillie is now an analyst for MLB Network?

    a. Jim Kaat
    b. Pedro Martinez
    c. Mike Schmidt
    d. Both A and B

15. Jake Arrieta was a groomsman in which MLB player's wedding?

    a. Kris Bryant
    b. Matt Carpenter
    c. Anthony Rizzo
    d. Adam Wainwright

16. Dale Sveum is the cousin of former Toronto Blue Jays player John Olerud.

    a. True
    b. False

17. Kyle Kendrick's wife Stephanie was a three-time contestant on which TV reality show?

    a. Big Brother
    b. American Ninja Warrior

c. Survivor

d. The Amazing Race

18. When he was a kid growing up in Las Vegas, Bryce Harper played baseball with which current MLB star?

a. Kris Bryant

b. Joey Gallo

c. Mike Trout

d. Both A and B

19. Early in his career, A.J. Burnett named his bats after songs by which musical artist(s)?

a. Panic! at the Disco

b. Marilyn Manson

c. Madonna

d. Michael Jackson

20. A species of weevil, *Sicoderus bautistai,* was named after José Bautista in 2018.

a. True

b. False

QUIZ ANSWERS

1. B – The Office

2. A – True

3. D – Vegas Golden Knights

4. C – Survivor

5. A – Hawaii Five-0

6. D – The Ellen DeGeneres Show

7. A – True

8. C – Harry Caray

9. B – Walt Disney World

10. C – Elvis

11. A – Albert Pujols

12. A – True

13. D – Jamie Lynn Sigler

14. D – Both A and B

15. B – Matt Carpenter

16. A – True

17. C – Survivor

18. D – Both A and B

19. B – Marilyn Manson

20. A – True

DID YOU KNOW?

1. Curt Schilling is one of only 11 players born in the state of Alaska to play in the MLB.

2. Shane Victorino and his family were on an episode of the show, *Tanked*. Brett Raymer and Wayde King made the family a baseball cap fish tank and installed it next to the staircase in their home.

3. Jim Thome established a fund during his playing days to help put his 10 nieces and nephews through college.

4. Hunter Pence appeared in an episode of *Fuller House*, playing himself. He also appeared on an episode of *Bill Nye Saves the World*.

5. In 2012, Jake Arrieta appeared on an episode of the HBO show, *Veep*. In 2017, he appeared in an episode of *Chicago Fire* alongside former teammate Kris Bryant.

6. During the 2008 season, as a member of the Detroit Tigers, Placido Polanco became a naturalized American citizen. He took his oath of citizenship during a pregame ceremony at Comerica Park.

7. Bryce Harper is known for hitting home runs on Opening Day. He became the first player in MLB history to hit five home runs in Opening Day games before the age of 25.

8. Roy Halladay was the first player to be inducted into the

National Baseball Hall of Fame posthumously since Roberto Clemente in 1973.

9. Bryce Harper has a dog named "Wrigley." The man clearly loves baseball.

10. Charlie Manuel has survived a heart attack, quadruple bypass surgery, kidney cancer, and a blocked, infected colon.

CHAPTER 10:

OUTFIELDERS

QUIZ TIME!

1. Raul Ibañez played the seasons with the Philadelphia Phillies. Which of the following teams did he NOT play for during his 19-season career?

    a. Seattle Mariners

    b. New York Yankees

    c. Minnesota Twins

    d. Kansas City Royals

2. Former Phillies left fielder Pat Burrell was never named to an MLB All-Star Game in his 12-year MLB career.

    a. True

    b. False

3. How many Gold Glove Awards did former Phillie Pete Rose win during his 24-year MLB career?

    a. 0

    b. 2

    c. 5

    d. 10

4. Marlon Byrd was named to only one MLB All-Star Game in his 15-year MLB career.

   a. True
   b. False

5. Jayson Werth played four seasons with the Philadelphia Phillies. Which of the following teams did he NOT play for during his 15-season career?

   a. Washington Nationals
   b. Texas Rangers
   c. Los Angeles Dodgers
   d. Toronto Blue Jays

6. Former Phillies left fielder Greg Luzinski played for two teams in his 15-season MLB career; the Phillies and which team?

   a. Cleveland Indians
   b. Arizona Diamondbacks
   c. Boston Red Sox
   d. Chicago White Sox

7. Shane Victorino played his entire 12-year MLB career with the Phillies.

   a. True
   b. False

8. How many seasons did outfielder Hunter Pence play for the Phillies?

   a. 1
   b. 2

c. 3

d. 4

9. How many home runs did Jayson Werth hit for the Phillies during the 2009 season?

   a. 24

   b. 27

   c. 36

   d. 44

10. How many seasons did outfielder Pat Burrell play for the Philadelphia Phillies?

    a. 2

    b. 5

    c. 7

    d. 9

11. John Kruk played for six seasons with the Philadelphia Phillies. He also played for the Chicago White Sox and which other team?

    a. San Diego Padres

    b. Los Angeles Dodgers

    c. Boston Red Sox

    d. Atlanta Braves

12. Marlon Byrd was named NL Rookie of the Year in 2003.

    a. True

    b. False

13. How many home runs did former Phillies outfielder Juan Pierre hit during his one season in Philadelphia?

a. 0

b. 1

c. 3

d. 5

14. How many games did John Mayberry play for the Phillies during his five seasons in Philadelphia?

    a. 300

    b. 400

    c. 500

    d. 600

15. How many bases did Pete Rose steal during his five years as a Phillie?

    a. 45

    b. 51

    c. 55

    d. 61

16. How many games did Jeff Francoeur play for the Phillies during the 2015 season?

    a. 99

    b. 101

    c. 110

    d. 118

17. How many times was former Phillie Pete Rose named to the MLB All-Star Game?

    a. 9 times

    b. 14 times

    c. 17 times

    d. 20 times

18. How many triples did Shane Victorino hit for the Phillies during the 2011 season?

    a. 16

    b. 15

    c. 14

    d. 13

19. How many seasons did Chuck Klein spend with the Philadelphia Phillies?

    a. 3 years

    b. 10 years

    c. 15 years

    d. 17 years

20. Lonnie Smith played for two MLB teams in his 17-season career; the Phillies and the Atlanta Braves.

    a. True

    b. False

QUIZ ANSWERS

1. C – Minnesota Twins

2. A – True

3. B – 2

4. A – True

5. B – Texas Rangers

6. D – Chicago White Sox

7. B – False [Boston Red Sox (3 years), Los Angeles Dodgers (1 year), San Diego Padres (1 year), Los Angeles Angels of Anaheim (1 year)]

8. B – 2

9. C – 36

10. D – 9

11. A – San Diego Padres

12. B – False (He finished in 4th place; Dontrelle Willis was named the NL Rookie of the Year.)

13. B – 1

14. C – 500

15. B – 51

16. D – 118

17. C – 17 times

18. A – 16

19. C – 15 years

20. B – False [Six teams: Atlanta Braves (5 years), Phillies (4 years), St. Louis Cardinals (4 years), Kansas City Royals (3 years), Baltimore Orioles (2 years), Pittsburgh Pirates (1 year)]

DID YOU KNOW?

1. Bryce Harper hit 35 home runs in his first season as a Phillie. He played in 157 games and collected 114 RBIs.

2. Pat Burrell played 1,306 games for the Philadelphia Phillies, the most of any team he played for during his 12-year MLB career. He also played for the Tampa Bay Rays and the San Francisco Giants.

3. Marlon Byrd played 410 games for the Phillies, the most of any team he played for during his 15-year MLB career. He also played for the Texas Rangers, Chicago Cubs, Washington Nationals, New York Mets, San Francisco Giants, Pittsburgh Pirates, Boston Red Sox, Cleveland Indians, and the Cincinnati Reds.

4. Greg Luzinski played 1,289 games total for the Philadelphia Phillies, the most of any team he played for during his 15-year MLB career. He also played for the Chicago White Sox.

5. Lenny Dykstra played 734 games total for the Philadelphia Phillies, the most of any team he played for during his 12-year MLB career. He also played for the New York Mets.

6. In his 24-season MLB career, Pete Rose was named MVP, Rookie of the Year, was a 17x All-Star, 3x World Series Champion, 2x Gold Glove Award winner, Silver

Slugger Award winner, World Series MVP, and he won three batting titles.

7. Lonnie Smith was a 1x All-Star and 3x World Series Champion. He played In 196 games during his four years in Philadelphia.

8. Jeff Francoeur played 118 games total for the Philadelphia Phillies. During his 12-season career, he also played for the Atlanta Braves, Kansas City Royals, New York Mets, San Francisco Giants, Texas Rangers, San Diego Padres, and the Miami Marlins.

9. Andrew McCutchen hit 10 home runs in his first season in Philly. He has also played for the Pittsburgh Pirates, New York Yankees, and the San Francisco Giants.

10. Bryce Harper was named the 2012 National League Rookie of the Year as a member of the Washington Nationals. He was also named to his first MLB All-Star Game that year.

CHAPTER 11:

INFIELDERS

QUIZ TIME!

1. Chase Utley played for two MLB teams during his 16-season career: the Phillies and which other team?

    a. Seattle Mariners
    b. Minnesota Twins
    c. San Diego Padres
    d. Los Angeles Dodgers

2. Mike Schmidt played his entire 18-season MLB career with the Phillies.

    a. True
    b. False

3. How many stolen bases did former Phillies shortstop Jimmy Rollins record during his 2001 season?

    a. 29
    b. 37
    c. 46
    d. 55

a. 2

b. 3

c. 5

d. 7

14. What college did former Phillies first baseman Travis Lee attend?

    a. Long Beach State University

    b. UC Berkeley

    c. UC Davis

    d. San Diego State University

15. How many Silver Slugger Awards did Chase Utley win during his 16-season MLB career?

    a. 2

    b. 4

    c. 6

    d. 8

16. Mike Schmidt was never named National League MVP.

    a. True

    b. False

17. What was Ryan Howard's batting average for the Phillies' 2008 championship season?

    a. .201

    b. .231

    c. .251

    d. .281

18. How many home runs did Jimmy Rollins hit during the Phillies' 2008 championship season?

    a. 11

    b. 22

    c. 33

    d. 44

19. What was Chase Utley's batting average during the Phillies' 2008 championship season?

    a. .280

    b. .287

    c. .292

    d. .332

20. Mike Schmidt hit 48 home runs during the Phillies' 1980 World Championship season.

    a. True

    b. False

QUIZ ANSWERS

1. D – Los Angeles Dodgers

2. A – True

3. C – 46

4. C – 58

5. B – San Diego Padres

6. C – 16

7. A – True

8. D – Chicago Cubs

9. B – 6

10. B – 1997

11. A – Manny Trillo

12. A – True

13. C – 5

14. D – San Diego State University

15. B – 4

16. B – False (He was a 3x MVP.)

17. C – .251

18. A – 11

19. C – .292

20. A – True

DID YOU KNOW?

1. Third baseman Mike Schmidt spent his entire 18-season career with the Philadelphia Phillies. He is a Hall-of-Famer, a 3x MVP, a 12x All-Star, a 1980 World Series Champion, a 10x Gold Glove Award winner, a 6x Silver Slugger Award winner, and a World Series MVP.

2. Second baseman Chase Utley played for the Philadelphia Phillies for 13 seasons and for the Los Angeles Dodgers for four seasons. He is a 6x All-Star, 4x Silver Slugger Award winner, and a 2008 World Series champion.

3. First baseman Ryan Howard spent his entire 13-season career with the Philadelphia Phillies. He is a 3x All-Star, 1x MVP, Rookie of the Year Award winner, Silver Slugger Award winner, NLCS MVP, Major League Player of the Year winner, and 2008 World Series champion.

4. Former Phillie José Bautista was a 6x All-Star and 3x Silver Slugger Award winner. He played for eight MLB teams during his 15-season career. In addition to the Phillies, he played for the Pittsburgh Pirates, Baltimore Orioles, Kansas City Royals, New York Mets, Tampa Bay Devil Rays, Toronto Blue Jays, and the Atlanta Braves.

5. Shortstop Larry Bowa played for the Philadelphia Phillies for 12 seasons, the Chicago Cubs for four seasons, and the New York Mets for one season. He is a

5x All-Star, 2x Gold Glove Award winner, Manager of the Year Award winner, and 1980 World Series Champion.

6. Infielder Dick Allen played for the Philadelphia Phillies for nine seasons, the Chicago White Sox for three seasons, the St. Louis Cardinals for one season, the Oakland A's for one season, and the Los Angeles Dodgers for one season. He is a 7x All-Star, Rookie of the Year Award winner, and 1x MVP.

7. Infielder Placido Polanco played for the Philadelphia Phillies for seven seasons, the St. Louis Cardinals for five seasons, the Detroit Tigers for five seasons, and the Miami Marlins for one season. He is a 2x All-Star, 3x Gold Glove Award winner, Silver Slugger Award winner, and ALCS MVP.

8. Infielder Ryne Sandberg played for the Philadelphia Phillies for one season and the Chicago Cubs for 15 seasons. He is a Hall-of-Famer, 10x All-Star, MVP, 9x Gold Glove Award winner, 7x Silver Slugger Award winner, and Major League Player of the Year.

9. Sparky Anderson spent only one season in MLB as a player. With the Phillies, he played 152 games in 1959 as a second baseman. He went on to be named to the National Baseball Hall of Fame as a manager and was a 2x Manager of the Year Award winner.

10. Former Phillie José Bautista won the 2010 and 2011 American League Hank Aaron Award. This award is given each season to the best hitter in each league.

CHAPTER 12:

PITCHERS AND CATCHERS

QUIZ TIME!

1. What was Steve Carlton's ERA during his 1980 World Series championship season with the Phillies?

    a. 2.04

    b. 2.34

    c. 2.64

    d. 2.84

2. Current Phillies manager Joe Girardi was a catcher during his MLB playing career.

    a. True

    b. False

3. How many All-Star Games was Carlos Ruiz named to in his 12-season career?

    a. 1

    b. 3

    c. 4

    d. 7

4. How many World Series championships did Curt Schilling win in his 20-season MLB career?

    a. 0

    b. 1

    c. 3

    d. 4

5. How many wins did pitcher Roy Halladay collect for the Phillies in 2010?

    a. 16

    b. 18

    c. 21

    d. 22

6. How many shutouts did Cole Hamels pitch as a member of the Phillies?

    a. 4

    b. 5

    c. 6

    d. 7

7. Former Phillies pitcher Robin Roberts was never named to an MLB All-Star Game in his playing career.

    a. True

    b. False

8. How many All-Star Games was former Phillies pitcher Cliff Lee named to in his playing career?

    a. 2

    b. 4

c. 6

d. 8

9. How many strikeouts did A.J. Burnett record with the Phillies in 2008?

    a. 170

    b. 180

    c. 190

    d. 200

10. What year was Jim Bunning named to the National Baseball Hall of Fame?

    a. 1993

    b. 1996

    c. 1997

    d. 1999

11. What was J.A. Happ's ERA for his 2009 season with the Phillies?

    a. 1.85

    b. 2.69

    c. 2.93

    d. 3.18

12. Pitcher Ryan Madson spent his entire 13-year MLB career with the Philadelphia Phillies.

    a. True

    b. False

13. Tug McGraw played for two teams during his 19-season MLB career; the Phillies and which other team?

a. Oakland A's

b. Texas Rangers

c. Los Angeles Dodgers

d. New York Mets

14. How many All-Star Games was former Phillies pitcher Jonathan Papelbon named to during his 12-season career?

   a. 6

   b. 7

   c. 8

   d. 9

15. How many strikeouts did Joe Blanton collect during his 2009 season with the Phillies?

   a. 133

   b. 143

   c. 153

   d. 163

16. Former Blue Jays catcher Mike Lieberthal hit 31 home runs in his 1999 season with the Phillies.

   a. True

   b. False

17. How many Gold Glove Awards did pitcher Jim Kaat win during his 25-season MLB career?

   a. 7

   b. 9

   c. 12

   d. 16

18. During his 19-year MLB career, Robin Roberts pitched for the Phillies, Houston Astros, Chicago Cubs, and

_____.

   a. Oakland A's

   b. New York Mets

   c. Baltimore Orioles

   d. Los Angeles Dodgers

19. How many saves did Brad Lidge collect for the Phillies during their 2008 championship season?

   a. 31

   b. 41

   c. 44

   d. 50

20. Roy Halladay won a Cy Young Award in 2010 as a member of the Philadelphia Phillies.

   a. True

   b. False

QUIZ ANSWERS

1. B – 2.34

2. A – True

3. A – 1

4. C – 3

5. C – 21

6. D – 7

7. B – False (7x All-Star)

8. B – 4

9. C – 190

10. B – 1996

11. C – 2.93

12. B – False (Oakland A's, Washington Nationals, Kansas City Royals, Los Angeles Dodgers)

13. D – New York Mets

14. A – 6

15. D – 163

16. A – True

17. D – 16

18. C – Baltimore Orioles

19. B – 41

20. A – True

DID YOU KNOW?

1. Carlos Ruiz is the only player in the history of the National League to catch four no-hitters and one of only two catchers to do it in MLB history.

2. Pitcher Roy Halladay played for the Philadelphia Phillies for four seasons and for the Toronto Blue Jays for 12 seasons. He is a Hall-of-Famer, 2x Cy Young Award winner, and an 8x All-Star. He also threw a perfect game as a member of the Phillies on May 29, 2010, against the Florida Marlins.

3. Pitcher Steve Carlton played for the Philadelphia Phillies for 15 seasons, the St. Louis Cardinals for seven seasons, the Minnesota Twins for two seasons, and the San Francisco Giants, the Cleveland Indians, and the Chicago White Sox for one season each. He is a Hall-of-Famer, 4x Cy Young Award winner, Triple Crown winner, 10x All-Star, Gold Glove Award winner, ERA title winner, and 2x World Series champion.

4. Pitcher Jim Bunning played for the Philadelphia Phillies for six seasons, the Detroit Tigers for nine seasons, the Pittsburgh Pirates for two seasons, and the Los Angeles Dodgers for one season. He is a Hall-of-Famer and 9x All-Star.

5. Pitcher Curt Schilling played for the Philadelphia Phillies for nine seasons, the Arizona Diamondbacks for

four seasons, the Boston Red Sox for four seasons, the Baltimore Orioles for three seasons, and the Houston Astros for one season. He is a 6x All-Star, World Series MVP, NLCS MVP, and 3x World Series champion.

6. The Phillies have had 13 no-hitters in franchise history. Two of them were perfect games. The no-hitters were thrown by Charles Ferguson, Red Donahue, Chick Fraser, Johnny Lush, Rick Wise, Terry Mulholland, Tommy Greene, Kevin Millwood, Roy Halladay, Cole Hamels/Jake Diekman/Ken Giles/Jonathan Papelbon (combined no-hitter), and Cole Hamels. The two perfect games were thrown by Jim Bunning and Roy Halladay.

7. Pitcher Grover Cleveland Alexander played for the Philadelphia Phillies for eight seasons, the Chicago Cubs for nine seasons, and the St. Louis Cardinals for four seasons. He is a Hall-of-Famer, 3x Triple Crown winner, 5x ERA Title winner, and 1926 World Series champion.

8. Pitcher Robin Roberts played for the Philadelphia Phillies for 14 seasons, the Baltimore Orioles for four seasons, the Houston Astros for two seasons, and the Chicago Cubs for one season. He is a Hall-of-Famer, Major League Player of the Year Award winner, and 7x All-Star.

9. Pitcher Tug McGraw played for the Philadelphia Phillies for 10 seasons and for the New York Mets for nine seasons. He is a 2x All-Star and 2x World Series Champion. His son is also a pretty successful country music artist.

10. Pitcher Cole Hamels has played for the Philadelphia Phillies for 10 seasons, the Texas Rangers for four seasons, and the Chicago Cubs for two seasons. So far, he is a 4x All-Star, NLCS MVP, World Series MVP, and 2008 World Series champion.

CHAPTER 13:

WORLD SERIES

QUIZ TIME!

1. How many World Series have the Philadelphia Phillies won in franchise history?

    a. 0

    b. 1

    c. 2

    d. 4

2. How many NL pennants have the Phillies won?

    a. 3

    b. 5

    c. 7

    d. 9

3. Which team did the Philadelphia Phillies face in the 1980 World Series?

    a. New York Yankees

    b. Oakland Athletics

    c. Minnesota Twins

    d. Kansas City Royals

4. Which team did the Phillies face in the 2008 World Series?

    a. Kansas City Royals
    b. Tampa Bay Rays
    c. Seattle Mariners
    d. Toronto Blue Jays

5. Who was the Phillies' manager during their 1980 World Series win?

    a. Danny Ozark
    b. Dallas Green
    c. Terry Francona
    d. Paul Owens

6. How many games were played in the 1980 World Series?

    a. 4
    b. 5
    c. 6
    d. 7

7. Mike Schmidt was named the 1980 World Series MVP.

    a. True
    b. False

8. Which Phillies player was named the 2008 World Series MVP?

    a. Shane Victorino
    b. Chase Utley
    c. Ryan Howard
    d. Cole Hamels

9. How many games did the 2008 World Series go?

    a. 4

    b. 5

    c. 6

    d. 7

10. Who was the Phillies manager when they won the 2008 World Series?

    a. Charlie Manuel

    b. Ryne Sandberg

    c. Larry Bowa

    d. Terry Francona

11. Which pitcher started Game 1 of the 2008 World Series for the Phillies?

    a. Brett Myers

    b. J.A. Happ

    c. Cole Hamels

    d. Joe Blanton

12. The Philadelphia Phillies lost the 1993 World Series to the Toronto Blue Jays.

    a. True

    b. False

13. Which Phillie hit the most home runs in the 1980 World Series?

    a. Pete Rose

    b. Bob Boone

    c. Bake McBride

    d. Mike Schmidt

14. Which Phillie hit the most home runs in the 2008 World Series?

    a. Chase Utley
    b. Ryan Howard
    c. Carlos Ruiz
    d. Jayson Werth

15. Which of the following Phillies did NOT hit a home run in the 2008 World Series?

    a. Jimmy Rollins
    b. Joe Blanton
    c. Eric Bruntlett
    d. Carlos Ruiz

16. The Philadelphia Phillies have never won a wild card berth.

    a. True
    b. False

17. Which team did the Philadelphia Phillies face in the 1980 NLCS to advance to the World Series?

    a. Florida Marlins
    b. Milwaukee Brewers
    c. Cincinnati Reds
    d. Houston Astros

18. Which team did the Philadelphia Phillies face in the 2008 NLCS to advance to the World Series?

    a. San Francisco Giants
    b. Los Angeles Dodgers

c. Washington Nationals

d. Chicago Cubs

19. What was the final score of Game 6 of the 1980 World Series?

    a. Phillies 9, Royals 6

    b. Phillies 2, Royals 0

    c. Phillies 4, Royals 1

    d. Phillies 8, Royals 4

20. What was the final score of Game 5 of the 2008 World Series?

    a. Phillies 7, Rays 6

    b. Phillies 6, Rays 5

    c. Phillies 5, Rays 4

    d. Phillies 4, Rays 3

QUIZ ANSWERS

1. C – 2
2. C – 7
3. D – Kansas City Royals
4. B – Tampa Bay Rays
5. B – Dallas Green
6. C – 6
7. A – True
8. D – Cole Hamels
9. B – 5
10. A – Charlie Manuel
11. C – Cole Hamels
12. A – True
13. D – Mike Schmidt (2)
14. B – Ryan Howard (3)
15. A – Jimmy Rollins
16. A – True
17. D – Houston Astros
18. B – Los Angeles Dodgers
19. C – Phillies 4, Royals 1
20. D – Phillies 4, Rays 3

DID YOU KNOW?

1. Steve Carlton's 17 strikeouts was the most by any pitcher in the 1980 World Series. Cole Hamels led all Phillies pitchers with 8 strikeouts in the 2008 World Series.

2. Both Taylor Swift and Patti LaBelle sang the National Anthem during the 2008 World Series.

3. Larry Bowa had the most hits for the Phillies in the 1980 World Series with 9 and Jayson Werth led the team in the 2008 World Series with 8 hits.

4. Steve Carlton had the most wins during the 1980 World Series with 2. J.C. Romero had the most wins during the 2008 World Series, also with 2.

5. The 1980 World Series took place from October 14 through October 21. The 2008 World Series took place from October 22 through October 27.

6. Mike Schmidt scored the most runs for the Phillies in the 1980 World Series with 6. Chase Utley scored the most runs for the Phillies in the 2008 World Series with 5.

7. Game 1 of the 1980 World Series was played in Veterans Stadium in Philadelphia. Eddie Sawyer threw out the first pitch and the All-Philadelphia Boys Choir and Mens Choir sang the National Anthem.

8. Game 6 of the 1980 World Series was also played at

Veterans Stadium. Tony Taylor threw out the first pitch and Charley Pride sang the National Anthem.

9. Game 1 of the 2008 World Series was played at Tropicana Field in Tampa, Florida. Bob Stewart threw out the first pitch and the boyband, the Backstreet Boys, sang the National Anthem.

10. Game 5 of the 2008 World Series was played at Citizens Bank Park in Philadelphia. Jim Bunning threw out the first pitch and John Oates from Hall and Oates sang the National Anthem.

CHAPTER 14:

HEATED RIVALRIES

QUIZ TIME!

1. Which team does NOT play in the National League East with the Phillies?

    a. Miami Marlins

    b. New York Mets

    c. Washington Nationals

    d. Baltimore Orioles

2. The Phillies are a founding member of the NL East Division.

    a. True

    b. False

3. Which team did NOT move from the NL East to the NL Central in 1994?

    a. Chicago Cubs

    b. Pittsburgh Pirates

    c. Toronto Blue Jays

    d. St. Louis Cardinals

4. The Phillies have won two World Series. How many have the New York Mets won?

   a. 0
   b. 2
   c. 4
   d. 5

5. The Phillies have won two World Series. How many have the Atlanta Braves won?

   a. 0
   b. 2
   c. 3
   d. 7

6. The Phillies have two World Series. How many have the Pittsburgh Pirates won?

   a. 0
   b. 2
   c. 3
   d. 5

7. The Phillies have won more NL East championships than any other team.

   a. True
   b. False

8. Which player has NOT played for both the Mets and the Phillies?

   a. Joe Blanton
   b. Bobby Abreu

c. Larry Bowa

d. Pedro Martinez

9. Which player has NOT played for both the Expos/ Nationals and the Phillies?

a. Bryce Harper

b. Howie Kendrick

c. Pete Rose

d. Scott Rolen

10. Which player has NOT played for both the Braves and the Phillies?

a. Terry Mulholland

b. Jayson Werth

c. Johnny Oates

d. Kenny Lofton

11. Which player has NOT played for both the Marlins and the Phillies?

a. A.J. Burnett

b. Placido Polanco

c. Raul Ibañez

d. Juan Pierre

12. "The City Series" was any series between the Philadelphia Phillies and the Philadelphia Athletics. When the A's moved to Kansas City in 1955, the City Series came to an end.

a. True

b. False

13. Which NL East team has NEVER won the NL East Division title?

    a. New York Mets
    b. Florida/Miami Marlins
    c. Montreal Expos/Washington Nationals
    d. Atlanta Braves

14. The NL East and what other division are the only two MLB divisions in which every team has won at least one World Series?

    a. American League West
    b. American League East
    c. American League Central
    d. American League West

15. As of the end of the 2020 season, the last time the Phillies won the division was 2011. When was the last time the New York Mets won the division?

    a. 2010
    b. 2012
    c. 2013
    d. 2015

16. The Montreal Expos won just one National League East title, in 1981.

    a. True
    b. False

17. As of the end of the 2020 season, the last time the Phillies won the division was 2011. When was the last time the Washington Nationals won the division?

a. 2012

b. 2014

c. 2017

d. 2019

18. Which National League East team did the Philadelphia Phillies play in the 1993 NLCS?

    a. Atlanta Braves

    b. New York Mets

    c. Florida Marlins

    d. Montreal Expos

19. The Phillies have two World Series. How many do the Philadelphia/Kansas City/Oakland Athletics have?

    a. 3

    b. 6

    c. 8

    d. 9

20. The Phillies, Mets, and Expos/Nationals are the only founding members that are still in the NL East.

    a. True

    b. False

QUIZ ANSWERS

1. D – Baltimore Orioles

2. A – True

3. C – Toronto Blue Jays

4. B – 2

5. C – 3

6. D – 5

7. B – False (Atlanta Braves have 14; Phillies have second most with 11.)

8. A – Joe Blanton

9. D – Scott Rolen

10. B – Jayson Werth

11. C – Raul Ibañez

12. A – True

13. B – Florida/Miami Marlins

14. C – American League Central

15. D – 2015

16. A – True

17. C – 2017

18. A – Atlanta Braves

19. D – 9

20. A – True (Braves were in NL West until 1994 and Marlins are an expansion team that joined in 1993.)

DID YOU KNOW?

1. From 1969 through 1993, the Philadelphia Phillies and the Pittsburgh Pirates together won more than half of the NL East Division titles (15 out of 25). They were also the only teams in the NL East who won consecutive titles during that span.

2. When the NL Central was created, the Braves were supposed to move and the Pirates were supposed to stay in the NL East. However, the Braves wanted to stay in a division with the Marlins. The Marlins offered to go to the NL Central, but the Pirates ultimately were the ones to change divisions.

3. The Phillies/Nationals rivalry became more ferocious when Bryce Harper decided to sign with the Phillies in 2019 after spending seven seasons in Washington.

4. There was no City Series between the A's and Phillies in 1901 and 1902 due to a legal battle between the National and American Leagues.

5. The Phillies won five consecutive NL East Division titles, from 2007 through 2011.

6. In NL East history, the Atlanta Braves have won the division 14 times, the Phillies 11 times, the Pirates nine times, the Mets six times, the Nationals five times, the Cardinals three times, and the Cubs two times. The Marlins have never won the division.

7. Joe Blanton, Marlon Byrd, Asdrubal Cabrera, Bryce Harper, Howie Kendrick, Brad Lidge, Pedro Martinez, Derrick May, Jonathan Papelbon, Pete Rose, Nate Schierholtz, Matt Stairs, Jayson Werth, and Jerome Williams have all played for both the Phillies and the Expos/Nationals.

8. Bobby Abreu, Rod Barajas, José Bautista, Larry Bowa, Marlon Byrd, Asdrubal Cabrera, Don Cardwell, Lenny Dykstra, Jeff Francoeur, Tug McGraw, and Jason Vargas have all played for both the Phillies and the New York Mets.

9. Peter Bourjos, José Bautista, Michael Bourn, Don Cardwell, Al Dark, Johnny Evers, Jeff Francoeur, Billy Hamilton, Kenny Lofton, Bob Uecker, Terry Mulholland, and Johnny Oates have all played for both the Phillies and the Atlanta Braves.

10. A.J. Burnett, Jeff Francoeur, John Mabry, Logan Morrison, Juan Pierre, Placido Polanco, J.T. Realmuto, Nate Robertson, and Jason Vargas have all played for both the Phillies and the Florida/Miami Marlins.

CHAPTER 15:

THE AWARDS SECTION

QUIZ TIME!

1. Which Phillies pitcher won the National League Cy Young Award in 2010?

    a. Cole Hamels

    b. Roy Halladay

    c. Jamie Moyer

    d. J.A. Happ

2. No Phillies first baseman has ever won a Gold Glove Award.

    a. True

    b. False

3. Which Phillies player won the National League MVP Award in 2007?

    a. Shane Victorino

    b. Chase Utley

    c. Ryan Howard

    d. Jimmy Rollins

4. Which Phillie most recently won the NL Rookie of the Year Award (as of the 2020 season)?

    a. Jack Sanford
    b. Dick Allen
    c. Ryan Howard
    d. Scott Rolen

5. How many NL Gold Glove Awards did Shane Victorino win during his time as a Phillie?

    a. 2
    b. 3
    c. 5
    d. 8

6. Who are the only two third basemen in Phillies franchise history to win Gold Glove Awards?

    a. Mike Schmidt and Scott Rolen
    b. Placido Polanco and Scott Rolen
    c. Mike Schmidt and Placido Polanco
    d. David Bell and Mike Schmidt

7. No Phillies manager has ever won the National League Manager of the Year Award.

    a. True
    b. False

8. Which Phillies player was named the DHL Hometown Hero (voted by MLB fans as the most outstanding player in franchise history)?

    a. Richie Ashburn
    b. Steve Carlton

c. Robin Roberts

d. Mike Schmidt

9. Who was the first Phillie named National League Rookie of the Year?

    a. Jack Sanford

    b. Dick Allen

    c. Scott Rolen

    d. Ryan Howard

10. In what year did Pete Rose win his sole Silver Slugger Award?

    a. 1979

    b. 1981

    c. 1982

    d. 1983

11. Which Phillie was named the Wilson MLB Defensive Player of the Year in 2012 and 2013?

    a. Chase Utley

    b. Hunter Pence

    c. Carlos Ruiz

    d. Shane Victorino

12. Jim Thome NEVER won a Silver Slugger Award during his time in Philadelphia.

    a. True

    b. False

13. Who is the only Phillies player ever to win the Hank Aaron Award?

a. Chase Utley

b. Mike Schmidt

c. Jimmy Rollins

d. Ryan Howard

14. Who is the only Phillies hitter ever to win an NL Triple Crown?

a. Chuck Klein

b. Mike Schmidt

c. Pete Rose

d. Scott Rolen

15. Who is the only Phillie ever to win the MLB Heart and Hustle Award?

a. Shane Victorino

b. Cole Hamels

c. Roy Halladay

d. Ryan Howard

16. No Phillies player has ever won the Home Run Derby.

a. True

b. False

17. Who is the only Phillies player ever to win the MLB Comeback Player of the Year Award?

a. J.A. Happ

b. Roy Halladay

c. Brad Lidge

d. Jayson Werth

18. Which of the Phillies listed below NEVER won a Roberto Clemente Award during their time in Philadelphia?

    a. Bobby Abreu
    b. Greg Luzinski
    c. Garry Maddox
    d. Jimmy Rollins

19. How many Gold Glove Awards did Mike Schmidt win in his 18-year career with the Phillies?

    a. 8
    b. 9
    c. 10
    d. 12

20. Former Phillies pitcher Grover Cleveland Alexander won an NL Pitching Triple Crown in back-to-back years, 1915 and 1916.

    a. True
    b. False

QUIZ ANSWERS

1. B – Roy Halladay

2. B – False, Bill White (1966)

3. D – Jimmy Rollins

4. C – Ryan Howard (2005)

5. B – 3

6. A – Mike Schmidt (1976, 1977, 1978, 1979, 1980, 1981, 1982, 1983, 1984, 1986) and Scott Rolen (1998, 2000, 2001)

7. B – False (Larry Bowa in 2001)

8. D – Mike Schmidt

9. A – Jack Sanford (1957)

10. B – 1981

11. C – Carlos Ruiz

12. A – True (He won one in 1996 when he was with the Cleveland Indians.)

13. D – Ryan Howard (2006)

14. A – Chuck Klein (1933)

15. C – Roy Halladay (2010)

16. B – False, Bobby Abreu (2005), Ryan Howard (2006)

17. C – Brad Lidge (2008)

18. A – Bobby Abreu

19. C – 10

20. A – True

DID YOU KNOW?

1. The Philadelphia Phillies have had four different pitchers win Cy Young Awards: Steve Carlton (1972, 1977, 1980, 1982), John Denny (1983), Steve Bedrosian (1987), and Roy Halladay (2010).

2. Jimmy Rollins is the only shortstop in Philadelphia Phillies franchise history ever to win an NL Silver Slugger Award.

3. Four Philadelphia Phillies have won the NL Rookie of the Year Award: Jack Sanford (1957), Dick Allen (1964), Scott Rolen (1997), and Ryan Howard (2005).

4. Roy Halladay won the ESPN ESPY Award for Best Major League Baseball Player in 2011 for his 2010 performance with the Phillies.

5. The Philadelphia Phillies have had five different players win the NL MVP Award: Chuck Klein (1932), Jim Konstanty (1950), Mike Schmidt (1980, 1981, 1986), Ryan Howard (2006), and Jimmy Rollins (2007).

6. Three Phillies players have been named the Rolaids Relief Man of the Year Award: Al Holland (1983), Steve Bedrosian (1987), and Brad Lidge (2008).

7. The only Phillies player ever to win the All-Star Game MVP Award was Johnny Callison in 1964.

8. Five Phillies players have been named NLCS MVP: Manny Trillo (1980), Gary Matthews (1983), Curt

Schilling (1993), Cole Hamels (2008), and Ryan Howard (2009).

9. Although Charlie Manuel is the Phillies' all-time winningest manager, he never won an NL Manager of the Year Award during his time in Philly.

10. The first Phillies player to win a Gold Glove Award was shortstop Bobby Wine in 1963.

CHAPTER 16:

THE CITY OF BROTHERLY LOVE

QUIZ TIME!

1. What was the Liberty Bell originally called?

    a. American Bell

    b. State House Bell

    c. USA Bell

    d. Philly Bell

2. The Walnut Street Theater was originally owned by Edwin Booth, John Wilkes Booth's brother.

    a. True

    b. False

3. Philly is known as what "Capital" of the United States?

    a. Agriculture

    b. Technology

    c. Sandwich

    d. Mural

4. People in Philadelphia consume how many times more pretzels each year, compared to the average American?

    a. 4
    b. 8
    c. 12
    d. 16

5. What percentage of America's population lives within five hours of Philadelphia, and what percentage of Americans live within a two-hour flight of Philadelphia?

    a. 5, 10
    b. 10, 30
    c. 20, 40
    d. 25, 60

6. Eastern State Penitentiary in Philadelphia once held which famous criminal?

    a. Al Capone
    b. "Slick Willie" Sutton
    c. Morris "The Rabbi" Bolber
    d. All of the Above

7. On the Liberty Bell, Pennsylvania is spelled with only one "N."

    a. True
    b. False

8. Which famous actor is from the City of Brotherly Love?

    a. Johnny Depp
    b. Tom Hanks

c. Will Smith

d. Robert Downey Jr.

9. What is the name of Philadelphia's NFL team?

   a. Philadelphia Eagles

   b. Philadelphia Chargers

   c. Philadelphia Cardinals

   d. Philadelphia Patriots

10. What is the name of Philadelphia's NBA team?

    a. Philadelphia Heat

    b. Philadelphia Warriors

    c. Philadelphia Magic

    d. Philadelphia 76ers

11. What is the name of Philadelphia's NHL team?

    a. Philadelphia Kings

    b. Philadelphia Penguins

    c. Philadelphia Flyers

    d. Philadelphia Lightning

12. Philadelphia's MLS team is called the Philadelphia Union.

    a. True

    b. False

13. Where in Philadelphia were the Declaration of Independence and the Constitution signed?

    a. Philadelphia City Hall

    b. Christ Church

c. Independence Hall

d. One Liberty Place

14. What building's steps were immortalized in the run up the stairs scene in the film "Rocky"?

    a. Philadelphia Museum of Art

    b. Independence Hall

    c. The Franklin Institute

    d. Rodin Museum

15. What is the name of the arena that the Philadelphia 76ers of the NBA and the Philadelphia Flyers of the NHL call home?

    a. Pepsi Center

    b. Wells Fargo Center

    c. United Center

    d. Smoothie King Center

16. What is the name of the stadium that the Philadelphia Eagles of the NFL call home?

    a. Lincoln Financial Field

    b. Nissan Stadium

    c. Ford Field

    d. Hard Rock Stadium

17. Which famous basketball player was born in Philadelphia?

    a. Lebron James

    b. Kobe Bryant

    c. Steph Curry

    d. Shaquille O' Neal

18. Philadelphia International Airport is 5 miles away from Citizens Bank Park. What is the Philadelphia International Airport's code?

    a. PHD

    b. PIA

    c. PIL

    d. PHL

19. One out of every how many doctors in the United States is trained in Philadelphia?

    a. 3

    b. 6

    c. 8

    d. 10

20. Central High School in Philadelphia is the only high school in America that can grant bachelor's degrees to its students.

    a. True

    b. False

QUIZ ANSWERS

1. B – State House Bell

2. A – True

3. D – Mural

4. C – 12

5. D – 25, 60

6. D – All of the Above

7. A – True

8. C – Will Smith

9. A – Philadelphia Eagles

10. D – Philadelphia 76ers

11. C – Philadelphia Flyers

12. A – True

13. C – Independence Hall

14. A – Philadelphia Museum of Art

15. B – Wells Fargo Center

16. A – Lincoln Financial Field

17. B – Kobe Bryant

18. D – PHL

19. B – 6

20. A – True

DID YOU KNOW?

1. Philadelphia was home to the first hospital, medical school, zoo, newspaper, soft pretzel, lager beer, cheesesteak, lending library, fire company, first naval shipyard in America, first mint in America, and the first general-use computer.

2. The first Republican National Convention was held at Philadelphia's Musical Fund Hall in June of 1856.

3. Bartram's Garden is the oldest botanical garden in North America. The Penn Museum is home to the largest Egyptian Sphynx in the Western Hemisphere.

4. The Mütter Museum is home to several oddities, including slices of Albert Einstein's brain, tissue from the body of John Wilkes Booth, a corpse that turned into soap, and a tumor removed from President Grover Cleveland.

5. As an April Fool's Day prank in 1996, Taco Bell took out a full-page ad in six major newspapers claiming they had purchased the Liberty Bell and renamed it the "Taco Liberty Bell." People were outraged, to say the least.... April Fool's!

6. "In West Philadelphia born and raised, On the playground is where I spent most of my days Chilling out, maxing, relaxing all cool and all shooting some b-

ball outside of the school, When a couple of guys who were up to no good started making trouble in my neighborhood I got in one little fight and my mom got scared and said "You're moving with your auntie and uncle in Bel-Air" – Lyrics to *The Fresh Prince of Bel-Air* theme song

7. The famous Philly Cheesesteak was created in 1930 by Pat Olivieri, who owned a hot dog stand. According to his grandnephew, the current owner of Pat's King of Steaks, it originally did not even have cheese on it. It was originally steak and onions on a hot dog bun. The provolone cheese was an addition a little over a decade later.

8. Around 50 tree seedlings traveled to space with the Apollo 14 mission. One of these "moon trees" was planted in Philly's Washington Square Park. When the tree began to die in 2011, the National Park Service replaced it with a clone.

9. Philadelphia is home to more impressionist paintings than any other city in the world, besides Paris. Philly also has a Rodin Museum, which makes the city the largest collector of the sculptor's work outside of Paris.

10. Of the 100 questions on the United States Citizenship Test, half of the answers can be found in Philadelphia. The city is like one huge American history lesson.

CHAPTER 17:

LEFTY

QUIZ TIME!

1. Where was Steve Carlton born?

    a. San Diego, California

    b. Miami, Florida

    c. Denver, Colorado

    d. Indianapolis, Indiana

2. Steve Carlton's full name is Steven Norman Carlton.

    a. True

    b. False

3. Steve Carlton played for the Philadelphia Phillies for 15 of the 24 seasons he was in MLB. He also played for the St. Louis Cardinals, Minnesota Twins, San Francisco Giants, Cleveland Indians, and which other team?

    a. San Diego Padres

    b. Chicago White Sox

    c. Florida Marlins

    d. Kansas City Royals

4. What year was Steve Carlton born?

    a. 1949
    b. 1947
    c. 1945
    d. 1944

5. What uniform number did Steve Carlton wear as a member of the Phillies?

    a. 32
    b. 34
    c. 36
    d. 38

6. How many strikeouts did Steve Carlton record during his 24 MLB seasons?

    a. 3,990
    b. 4,001
    c. 4,136
    d. 4,583

7. Steve Carlton NEVER threw a no-hitter.

    a. True
    b. False

8. Steve Carlton is a 2x World Series Champion. He won a title in 1980 with the Phillies and another in 1967 with which team?

    a. Minnesota Twins
    b. Cleveland Indians
    c. St. Louis Cardinals
    d. Chicago White Sox

9. What college did Steve Carlton attend?

    a. Florida State University

    b. Miami Dade College

    c. University of Florida

    d. University of Miami

10. How many All-Star Games was Steve Carlton named to?

    a. 10

    b. 13

    c. 18

    d. 21

11. How many Gold Glove Awards did Steve Carlton win?

    a. 9

    b. 3

    c. 1

    d. 0

12. Steve Carlton committed 90 balks in his career, the most in MLB history.

    a. True

    b. False

13. What year was Steve Carlton inducted into the National Baseball Hall of Fame with 95.82% of the vote?

    a. 1993

    b. 1994

    c. 1995

    d. 1996

14. What year did Steve Carlton win a Pitching Triple Crown?

    a. 1970

    b. 1972

    c. 1974

    d. 1976

15. How many National League Cy Young Awards did Steve Carlton win?

    a. 1

    b. 2

    c. 3

    d. 4

16. Steve Carlton was the National League ERA leader in 1972.

    a. True

    b. False

17. How many times did Steve Carlton lead the National League in wins?

    a. 1

    b. 3

    c. 4

    d. 7

18. How many times Steve Carlton lead the National League in strikeouts?

    a. 1

    b. 3

c. 4

d. 5

19. What year did the Phillies retire Steve Carlton's No. 32?

    a. 1987

    b. 1989

    c. 1994

    d. 1998

20. In 2004, the Phillies unveiled a statue of Steve Carlton at Citizens Bank Park.

    a. True

    b. False

QUIZ ANSWERS

1. B – Miami, Florida

2. A – True

3. B – Chicago White Sox

4. D -1944

5. A – 32

6. C – 4,136

7. A – True

8. C – St. Louis Cardinals

9. B – Miami Dade College

10. A – 10

11. C – 1 (1981)

12. A – True

13. B – 1994

14. B – 1972

15. D – 4

16. A – True

17. C – 4 (1972, 1977, 1980, 1982)

18. D – 5 (1972, 1974, 1980, 1982, 1983)

19. B – 1989

20. A – True

DID YOU KNOW?

1. Steve Carlton has the most career strikeouts and the second-most career wins for any left-handed pitcher in MLB history.

2. Steve Carlton threw a whopping 30 complete games in his 1972 season with the Phillies. His ERA that year was 1.97 and he won 27 games. This was his first season in Philadelphia. He led the league in wins, ERA, innings pitched, and strikeouts. He also won his first Cy Young Award this season.

3. "Lefty was a craftsman, an artist. He was a perfectionist. He painted a ballgame. Stroke, stroke, stroke, and when he got through, it was a masterpiece." – Richie Ashburn

4. Steve Carlton made his MLB debut against the Chicago Cubs and played his final game against the Cleveland Indians.

5. Steve Carlton finished his career with a 329-244 record. His career ERA was 3.22. He appeared in 741 games, started 709 of them, earned 2 saves, and pitched a total of 5,217.2 innings.

6. Steve Carlton got the win in both Game 2 and Game 6 of the 1980 World Series. He pitched 15 innings, gave up 14 hits, struck out 17, and gave up 4 earned runs in his two starts.

7. Steve Carlton one struck out 19 Mets batters in one game…. and lost.

8. Carlton appeared in an episode of *Married… with Children*. He played himself.

9. "Why do you think you were put on this earth?" – ESPN's Roy Firestone

   "To teach the world how to throw a slider." – Steve Carlton's response

10. "Trying to get a hit off of Carlton is] like trying to drink coffee with a fork" – Hall-of-Famer Willie Stargell

CHAPTER 18:

J – ROLL

QUIZ TIME!

1. Where was Jimmy Rollins born?

   a. Madison, Wisconsin
   b. Philadelphia, Pennsylvania
   c. Detroit, Michigan
   d. Oakland, California

2. Jimmy Rollins is the cousin of Tony Tarasco, who played in the majors from 1993 to 2002.

   a. True
   b. False

3. Jimmy Rollins played for three teams during his 17-season MLB career: the Phillies, the Chicago White Sox, and which other team?

   a. Washington Nationals
   b. St. Louis Cardinals
   c. Los Angeles Dodgers
   d. Oakland Athletics

4. What year was Jimmy Rollins born?

    a. 1975
    b. 1978
    c. 1980
    d. 1983

5. How many MLB All-Star Games was Jimmy Rollins named?

    a. 3
    b. 6
    c. 7
    d. 10

6. What year was Jimmy Rollins named the National League MVP?

    a. 2001
    b. 2003
    c. 2005
    d. 2007

7. Jimmy Rollins appeared in several MC Hammer music videos when he was young.

    a. True
    b. False

8. How many Gold Glove Awards did Jimmy Rollins win?

    a. 2
    b. 4
    c. 8
    d. 12

9. What year did Jimmy Rollins win his sole Silver Slugger Award?

    a. 2005
    b. 2006
    c. 2007
    d. 2008

10. What MLB team was Jimmy Rollins a fan of when he was growing up?

    a. Philadelphia Phillies
    b. San Francisco Giants
    c. Los Angeles Dodgers
    d. Oakland A's

11. In what year did Jimmy Rollins win a Roberto Clemente Award?

    a. 2011
    b. 2012
    c. 2014
    d. 2015

12. Jimmy Rollins spent 15 out of the 17 seasons of his MLB career with the Philadelphia Phillies.

    a. True
    b. False

13. How many career home runs did Jimmy Rollins hit?

    a. 201
    b. 231
    c. 281
    d. 301

14. What year did Jimmy Rollins lead the National League in stolen bases?

    a. 2001
    b. 2005
    c. 2008
    d. 2011

15. How many stolen bases did Jimmy Rollins collect during the 2001 season?

    a. 31
    b. 36
    c. 46
    d. 50

16. Jimmy Rollins won the 2001 NL Rookie of the Year Award.

    a. True
    b. False

17. How many games did Jimmy Rollins play in for the Phillies during the 2007 season?

    a. 150
    b. 155
    c. 160
    d. 162

18. What is Jimmy Rollins' full name?

    a. Rutherford James Rollins
    b. Timothy James Rollins
    c. James Peter Rollins
    d. James Calvin Rollins

19. In his MLB debut, Rollins played against the Florida Marlins. His final game in the MLB was against the _____.

   a. Arizona Diamondbacks
   b. Milwaukee Brewers
   c. Washington Nationals
   d. Colorado Rockies

20. Jimmy Rollins retained his role as the Phillies' leadoff hitter for almost a full decade.

   a. True
   b. False

QUIZ ANSWERS

1. D – Oakland, California

2. A – True

3. C – Los Angeles Dodgers

4. B – 1978

5. A – 3

6. D – 2007

7. A – True

8. B – 4

9. C – 2007

10. D – Oakland A's

11. C – 2014

12. A – True

13. B – 231

14. A – 2001

15. C – 46

16. B – False (He came in 3rd; Albert Pujols won the award.)

17. D – 162

18. D – James Calvin Rollins

19. C – Washington Nationals

20. A – True

DID YOU KNOW?

1. In 2019, the Phillies hired Jimmy Rollins as a special advisor to the team. He was also an on-air commentator for a few Phillies games. He was honored in 2019 with a retirement ceremony. Although his No. 11 is not formally retired by the Phillies, they do keep it out of rotation in his honor.

2. Jimmy and his wife Johari established the Johari and Jimmy Rollins Center for Animal Rehabilitation in New Jersey. It offers rehab services and medical help to animals in need.

3. Jimmy Rollins holds an annual BaseBowl charity bowling tournament with proceeds benefitting the Arthritis Foundation.

4. Jimmy Rollins actively campaigned for Barack Obama in the 2008 election.

5. Jimmy Rollins is an investor in the eSports company, NRG Esports. Other NRG Esports investors include Alex Rodriguez, Ryan Howard, Shaquille O' Neal, Michael Strahan, Marshawn Lynch, and Jennifer Lopez.

6. In 2016, Jimmy Rollins signed a minor-league contract with the San Francisco Giants but was released right before the season began.

7. Jimmy Rollins admired Rickey Henderson while

growing up and tried to emulate him at the plate and in the way in which he played the game.

8. In 2014, Jimmy Rollins was traded from the Phillies to the Los Angeles Dodgers. Rollins waived his no-trade clause to make the move possible.

9. Jimmy Rollins was the first Phillies shortstop to win a Gold Glove Award since Larry Bowa in 1978.

10. Jimmy Rollins was the first player in MLB history to record 200 hits, 30 home runs, 20 triples, and 30 stolen bases in a single season.

CONCLUSION

Learn anything new? Now you truly are the ultimate Phillies fan! Not only did you learn about the Phillies of the modern era but you also expanded your knowledge back to the days of the 1980 and 2008 World Series championships.

You learned about the Phillies' origins, their history, and where they came from. You learned about the history of their uniforms and jersey numbers, you identified some famous quotes, and read some of the craziest nicknames of all time. You learned more about powerhouse hitter, Mike "Schmitty" Schmidt, Steve "Lefty" Carlton, and Jimmy "J-Roll" Rollins. You were amazed by Phillies stats and recalled some of the most famous Phillies trades and drafts/draft picks of all time. You broke down your knowledge by outfielders, infielders, pitchers, and catchers. You looked back on the Phillies championships and playoff feats and the awards that came before, after, and during them. You also learned about the Phillies' fiercest rivalries both within and outside their division.

Every team in the MLB has a storied history, but the Phillies have one of the most memorable of all. They have won two incredible World Series championships with the backing of their devoted fans. Being the ultimate Phillies fan takes knowledge and a whole lot of patience, which you tested with this book. Whether you knew every answer or were stumped by several questions, you learned some of the most interesting history that the game of baseball has to offer.

The history of the Phillies represents what we all love about the game of baseball. The heart, the determination, the tough times, and the unexpected moments, plus the players that inspire us and encourage us to do our best because, even if you get knocked down, there is always another game and another day.

With players like Bryce Harper, Andrew McCutchen, and Jake Arrieta, the future for the Phillies continues to look bright. There is no doubt that this franchise will continue to be one of the most competitive teams in Major League Baseball year after year.

It's a new decade, which means there is a clean slate, ready to continue writing the history of the Philadelphia Phillies. The ultimate Phillies fans cannot wait to see what's to come for their beloved Phils.

Made in the USA
Middletown, DE
11 December 2021

55244984R00089